SPELLBOUND Scones

FLEUR DEVILLAINY

To everyone
whose mouth waters
over the taste of
fresh scones...

or wolf shifters.

TRIGGER WARNINGS

Your mental health is important.

Spellbound Scone is a new adult paranormal romance intended for individuals 18+ years old and may not be suitable for all ages.

This book includes the following trigger warnings: open door sexual activity, fighting, and mild profanity

CHAPTER 1
NETTI

The moon hangs in the sky, casting an eerie glow through the shop's windows. The air is heavy with autumn magic, creating the perfect atmosphere for witchy mischief. I, however, find myself with an unexpected splatter of frosting on my chest.

"Netti Ellsworth," I grumble to myself as I hang my head and brace my hands on the rim of the industrial-sized Kitchen Aid mixer that has showered half its contents of buttercream frosting across my new dress and the bakery's floor. "You had one job."

The digital face of my watch lights up in a flash of yellow as I brush it against my apron. The glowing face beams back 18:35; an hour and a half still before closing. The sweet aroma of freshly baked pastries hangs heavy in the air as I work the closing shift—a solitary figure preparing for the next morning's frenzy. While the bakery, Magickal Morsels, is known for its enchanted baked goods, we also cater delicious treats to the locals for breakfast at the local coffee shop, EnchanTea.

The weight of my looming exam tomorrow and my overdue assignment—due before midnight—keeps me from falling into the relaxing rhythm of the closing tasks. It's been almost three years since I left home and moved to Rusthollow to pursue my nursing degree, and I am only a semester and a half from graduating. I glance around the kitchen, from the cooling cupcakes I was preparing to frost down to the sticky sweet splattering covering every viable kitchen surface.

"At least it's Wednesday," I muse, blowing a strand of pink hair out of my face.

Wednesday, our least busiest day. The likelihood I would be disturbed was small. Grabbing a damp rag, I clean the counters, the cool, smooth surface of the wood feeling good under my fingers. As a descendant of elemental witches, I always feel a surge of power when near wood, plants, or dirt, a connection to my magic that ran deep in my veins. It's one of the reasons I applied to the bakery when I first moved to the rustic town with its dense forest and small lake. From the moment I walked past the wooden sign into the cozy brick building, I felt at home.

I glance around me. The bookshelves, crammed with jars of dried herbs and books for customers to peruse, line the walls, adding a whimsical charm to the space. The kitchen has a large cast-iron stove and butcher block island counters.

That's when I spot the mop propped up against the pantry door from the corner of my eye.

Netti, to magic, there is balance. My mother's voice resonates in my head.

"What's the point of being a witch if I can't use magic to my advantage?" The corners of my lips curl into a feline grin. I grab the wooden handle between my palms and close my eyes.

My palms heat as I reach inside myself for the flickering kernel of magic.

HEART OF WOOD

TOOL of good

TO ALEVE DISTRESS

CLEAN UP this mess

THE WOOD beneath my palms seems to vibrate with energy.

Peeking open an eye, I wait with bated breath.

Seconds tick by.

Nothing.

I sigh, prop the mop back against the wall, and turn back to the counters.

This is why I left home. This is why I was pursuing a degree in nursing. Although I could tap into my magical abilities, I've never been able to wield them with great precision. I could bake up a spell or potion, but when it comes to incantation and levitation—our family's greatest legacy—I can hardly spell a thistle to roll over. Mom had tried to convince me to stay and learn the family way, but I was too stubborn and frustrated to study ancient magic and take over the bookstore. I love books, but I want to make a difference. I want to be there for those who are in need of help.

So when my best friend since elementary told me she'd

been accepted to a university out of state, I knew it was my sign to break out of my shell.

And look where I am now.

Working in a witch-owned bakery by day and going to nursing school by night.

Keeping up with friends and a love life? I snort. As if.

I hardly have time for my studies and extra shifts to pay my half of the rent. Love is on the back burner of my stove. And that doesn't even begin to touch the student loans stacking up. But the end is in sight. There is only a semester and a half left, and then I' be able to use my knowledge and skills for the good of others.

The little bell above the door rings, and I turn to face the front door. I can't imagine who is coming in this late at night, but hopefully, they won't linger.

"Welcome to Magickal Morsels," I say in my sweetest customer service voice as I plaster a smile on my face. After spending nearly the last two years working in the bakery, I knew almost every person who lived in town, their families, and the season regulars.

The little bakery, nestled in the heart of a picturesque town, was a hub of activity and a gathering place for locals and tourists alike. The scent of freshly baked bread and pastries always filled the air, creating an inviting atmosphere that drew people in. As I greeted the customers, I couldn't help but notice the familiarity in their faces and the warmth in their smiles.

However, today is different. The stranger walks in, catching my attention with his striking presence, and I can't help but feel as though I know him. His piercing blue eyes meet mine as he turns, and my heart stutters. I'm certain that I've never seen this man before, but I can't seem to shake the familiarity I feel. He holds my gaze for what feels like an age, the silence only broken by the ticking of the clock, before he finally breaks away. He rakes a hand through his short, dark hair as he silently surveys the quaint front room from our cozy brick walls to our picked-over display of pastries. The man reeks of money and business, from his pristine suit jacket to his polished shoes. The only thing standing out is a warm grey knitted scarf around his neck.

"Is there something I can help you with?" I ask, flashing him a smile.

His eyes land on me, and I feel the heat of his gaze as it rakes from my head to my toes, and suddenly the breath leaves my lungs. He steps up to our display counter, lips pressing together disapprovingly as he silently observes our dismal display of goods, ignoring me. The moment hangs in the air, and I can't help but wonder what brought this mysterious man to our humble bakery and what could possibly impress him.

"I'm afraid with it being fall break, the college kids picked us pretty clean today. If you know what you have in mind, I can put in a custom order for pick up—"

"This is Magickal Morsels?" He leans forward, his gaze intense as he asks. His hands rest firmly on the countertop. Something hot coils in my gut as he doesn't break eye contact.

"Well, yes, that's what I said." From the short distance, I can smell the woodsy scent of summer nights in the forests. I shake my head and fidget with the edge of my apron.

"I've heard you sell spelled pastries," he says, his eyes following my every movement like a predator.

"Well, that is what we're known for." My eyebrows draw together, but I step back, opening my arms wide. "What did you have in mind?"

His nostrils flare, and I could have sworn his pupils dilate until they nearly cover his irises, but in a split second, they are back to their cerulean blue.

"You have a little something—" He leans over the small

glass counter and runs his finger along my collarbone. Heat prickles my skin, and I think I couldn't possibly feel any hotter when he pulls back, holding up his finger, now smeared with white buttercream. The oven catching on fire couldn't have made this room any more suffocating than how I feel with the way he's looking at me.

"I, uhm." Nibbling my bottom lip, I glance behind me at the nearly-cleaned kitchen. "There was a little accident, just some buttercream frosting. But don't worry, it doesn't happen often, and I wouldn't dare feed spilled frosting to a customer. We pride ourselves on our pastries. Oh gosh, I'm rambling. I'm so sorry."

"Buttercream, you say?" He glances at his finger before licking the digit clean. His eyebrows raise a fraction. "Not bad."

I could have died then and there. How could one man make eating frosting so sexy?

Get a hold of yourself. You seriously need to get laid. I chide myself.

Honey stretches his wings from where he's been sleeping nestled against my hair bun, and a growl resonates deep within the stranger's chest, drawing his attention to my fruit bat.

"What is—that," he says pointedly. Honey stiffens atop my head and lets out a small growl at the stranger.

'It's just... it's just my familiar. He's a fruit bat," I blurt.

"Clearly."

"You—you said you were looking for something in particular?" I ask, trying to keep my voice from rising to a new octave and turning the conversation.

"Yes, I have a meeting tomorrow, and it won't do me any good to be distracted," he says huskily. He glances away from my hair, down at my plastic name tag pinned to my apron, with a sense of authority in his gaze. "Would it, Netti?" he asks, his tone implying that the answer should be obvious.

Who was this man to think I knew what his plans were or how he should behave?

Heat flushes across my cheeks and down my neck. I can't help but feel a bit intimidated by his intense gaze—as if I were a lamb facing off against a lion, completely outmatched. He raises an eyebrow, his polished leather shoes tapping impatiently on the tile floor, a clear sign that he is in a hurry.

"We have a variety of different things–" I begin, trying to sound helpful and cheery as I walk along the edge of the counter. My eyes roam over the nearly empty shelves, with neat little sold-out signs nestled in the crumbs. He follows my every move, his movements purposeful and predatory.

"Lemon tarts for luck, cinnamon rolls for confidence..." I trail off, realizing those items sold out after the morning rush. "I'm sorry. It looks like we sold the last of them." Besides, this man exudes enough confidence that it is the last thing he needs. Why did he need a spelled pastry, anyway? For that matter, why did anyone? The magic in them was not strong enough to truly change one's future, just enough to boost their natural feelings.

I continue along the display case, a coil of unease curling in my gut over disappointing a man I just met. *Get a hold of yourself, Netti.*

"I don't have all night," he says, his frustration evident as he crosses his arms over his chest and shifts his weight. I can't help but feel a sense of guilt, knowing I can't fulfill his request.

"I'm sorry," I finally say, mustering the courage to lift my eyes to his. A chill runs across my skin as I see the determination in his face. "We usually sell out of our most popular items before lunchtime. It seems luck and confidence are in high demand these days." I shrug sheepishly and smile at him.

"What *do* you have?" He meets my gaze with cold blue eyes, unimpressed by my ability to usually win over even the most unruly of customers. There is something wild and hungry in how he looks at me, which terrifies and excites me.

"Mini pecan pies for prosperity, a few macaroons for various ailments..." I trail off, ticking off on my fingers as I scan the shelves again. "Fudge for happiness, a few danishes that will–"

"No. None of those will do. I need something to help me focus, and that's it."

What he needed was a concentration scone. Those were some of the first things I learned to make when I first got hired because I knew they'd come in handy when studying. I glance at the nearly empty glass shelves, then back at the watch on my wrist. 19:40. Where had the last hour gone?

"We don't have what you're looking for–" I twirl a loose strand of my pink hair that had fallen from my twin buns while I nervously chew my bubble gum.

"But?"

My eyes widen as the gum pops, and he stares at me with pursed lips.

"What you need is a scone for concentration. I can have them ready first thing when we open at 05:00," I blurt out.

"That would please me very much," he says, the corners of his lips turning up into a wolfish grin as he leans over the counter. The way he looks at me turns my insides to molten chocolate and cause my ears to burn.

"How many are you looking to purchase?" I pull the notepad from my pocket and begin jotting down notes, anything to distract myself from staring into his eyes.

"How many do you think I'll need, Netti?" His voice is smooth, rich, and husky, like hot cocoa on a cold winter's night.

"Well, all you need is one, but they only last a few hours, so it depends on how long your meeting is and if–"

"I'll take a half dozen," he says without question or hesitation.

"The only question is… vanilla or lemon?"

I avert my eyes from his intense stare, my gaze falling to the warm, comforting texture of the wooden floor. His warm, calloused hand cups under my chin, and I feel the pressure of his touch as he raises my face to meet his eyes.

"Well, Netti, why don't you surprise me?"

I open my mouth to respond, but my voice seems to have deserted me. This was a new experience, as I usually jump in and fill the gaps in a conversation.

"That is, as long as they do their job," he says, laying a one-hundred-dollar bill on the counter. "Just make sure they're ready by 05:00. I don't like to be disappointed." He turns on his heel, his leather soles clicking softly on the tile.

"But sir–" I stare at the bill on the counter, enough for a half dozen orders at least. My face still tingles from the absence of his touch.

"It's Connor. Connor Abernathy. Keep the change… Netti." He glances at me one more time before the door clicks closed behind him, followed by a jingle of the bell.

My breath escapes my lungs in a rush, finally releasing the tension I hadn't noticed I was holding, and I let my weight settle against the cool countertop. Honey squeaks in protest from where he's nestled against my hair buns.

"Sorry." I reach up and stroke his dark, velvety snout before turning and facing the kitchen. I was going to need a double-shot espresso to get everything done in the next four hours.

CHAPTER 2
CONNOR

S he smelled good. I bet she would taste just as creamy and sweet as that frosting.

"Now is not the time and place for that," I grumble at my inner wolf as I inhale the fresh air, so different from the city I've grown accustomed to. The nearly full moon lights up the pavement like a beacon as I make my way down the sidewalk to my parked dark blue sports car rental.

I like it here. I like her.

"Of course you do. You like anything with two legs and the outdoors." I slide into the leather seats and punch in the address to the bed and breakfast I'm staying at. My body relaxes as the car connects to my phone and modern cello covers start playing. Tomorrow I am meeting the CEO of Summit Contracting Group to discuss the business proposal. I don't know why he insisted on meeting in a small town when it would have been more convenient to meet in the city where both our company's headquarters are.

Yes, you do. He says it's better for his health to get away from the city. I agree with him.

"Could you go back to being quiet?" I stare at the glowing orb in the sky. He was never this verbal when I was living with the pack, usually only nudging feelings my way. And those feelings usually only had to do with fighting, fucking, and eating. It had to be the combination of the upcoming full moon and being so far in the forest in this small town.

Will she be there tomorrow?

My mind goes to the girl at the bakery. I couldn't keep my eyes off her pale skin, bubblegum pink hair, and that damned frosting splattered all over her chest. The lingering scent of vanilla beans clings to my clothes from the short period of being in her presence. I grip the steering wheel until my knuckles blanch and focus on the moonlit road before me, following the GPS's directions.

"Not likely, with her working the closing shift." The road is crowded with single and double-story buildings, their front windows displaying a variety of different goods. Despite being a small town and lacking the larger luxuries of known chain stores, there seems to be a shop for every need. Even though it is late, the streets are still filled with people, their movements a blur in the dim street lights as I drive.

I pull into the neat row of parking spots in front of the Victorian-style building and turn off the ignition.

This meeting has to go right. With the plans for the condo expansion, this deal would put Abernathy Inc. on a whole new level. It would open up opportunities not only for homes for the expanding pack but hundreds of jobs for other humans and those in the magical community.

I thought you didn't care about the pack.

"I care about the pack. It's just messy." My chest constricts at the internal need to protect and provide. I had stepped away from the pack when my twin and I transitioned into adults and found ourselves equally matched, our internal wolves at each other's throats, vying to lead the pack as Alpha.

It wasn't messy. You just didn't fight, but you also didn't want to play beta to Carter.

"Carter is a good leader. He's done a perfectly fine job as Alpha." I rake my hand through my hair. I miss the days before our father died when we could be a family instead of being ruled by our animal instincts.

If he would have knelt and acknowledged you as Alpha, we never would have needed to leave the pack.

"His wolf would never have knelt to us. You know as well as I that Carter and I were equally matched in everything." Except people skills. He always was more of a charmer, knowing exactly what to say in every situation while I was the calm observer.

I beg to differ. You never gave us a fighting chance.

"I had other goals, and letting Carter stand in father's footsteps allowed us to step out from under the pack responsibilities and pursue other opportunities. I'd have never been able to start this company if I spent my days running the clan." I heave a heavy sigh.

You would have been a better leader for your people, especially with Carter as your beta. You were their protector. He would have been fine playing his part at your side.

Ignoring him, I open the door and inhale the fresh pine air. If I wasn't playing protector from afar, I would be happy living somewhere like this.

My phone vibrates, and I pull it out of my pocket. The screen lights up with a message from my secretary, Daisy.

Just confirming your meeting with Summit Contracting Group at tomorrow at 10:00.

That is correct. Thank you.

Your jet is ready to leave Friday evening at 18:00. You have a meeting with the board to go over the plans for the condo expansion on Monday at 08:00.

That sounds right.

Hope your trip goes smoothly. Although I wish you'd stay a little longer and just enjoy yourself and relax for once. Are you sure you don't want to take a few extra days off while you're away from the chaos of the city? I could push back the board meeting? You deserve the break.

Thanks, but keep things as planned. I'll see you in the office.

I TUCK my phone back into my pocket. Grabbing my bag and suitcase, I make my way to the private entrance to my rooms. The whitewashed door opens on silent hinges, and I'm hit with the aroma of vanilla. It immediately takes my mind back to the bakery and her damnable green eyes. I shake my head as I begin unloading my immaculately pressed and packed clothes, ready for the next two days. I can't afford to be distracted for this meeting, but maybe if all goes well, I could take a few needed days off. Daisy is always telling me that I'm working too hard and that I'm going to work myself to death. She has been with my company from the ground up, and even after her husband had passed, she continued to work for me. She said it kept her mind busy, and someone had to look after me.

THE SUN COLORS the sky in faint pastels as I push open the door to the bakery and am assaulted with the smell of fresh roasted coffee and an assortment of baked goods.

"Welcome to Magickal Morsels! How can I help you?" A tall blonde with tanned skin and curves calls out from behind the counter. Disappointment curls in my gut at the hopes that the petite pink-haired baker would be here this morning, but I brush the thought away and proceed to the counter.

"Yes, I have an order for scones for Connor Abernathy." My foot taps impatiently as I glance at my watch.

"Oh yes, Netti said she finished those last night before closing. One moment." She turns and makes her way into the back of the bakery and appears a few moments later carrying a small white box tied with a neat purple ribbon with my name written in neat curling script.

She stayed up thinking of us.

I scowl and take the box from her hands.

"Is there anyth–"

"No," I say and head for the door. It opens with a tingle of that damned bell, and an elderly man steps through.

"You're welcome," she says. "Oh, good morning, Mr. Claymont. You're looking particularly fetching this morning."

The old man's face lights up at her greeting, straightening his scarf before nodding at me as he passes. I push past him into the rising sunlight and am hit with the scent of sweet lemon frosting as the box crushes in my grip.

My mouth begins to water as I think back to the sweet taste of buttercream from last night and the girl.

"Get a hold of yourself, Connor."

Or you could get a hold of some locks of pink hair...

"No one asked for your opinion. I need coffee and time to concentrate." I set the box on the passenger seat, close the door, and head to the coffee shop before I return to my B&B. I have exactly three hours until I meet with Mr. Rogers.

Wrapping the towel around my waist, I lean over the sink and wipe the steam from the mirror and stare at my reflection. My dark locks fall over tanned skin, and my dark blue eyes stare back at me. My mind reels between the new project, this meeting, the upcoming full moon, and the pack before landing on the girl. Netti.

I shake my head and push away from the counter. She is just some witch in this small town. There are plenty of women back at home I could call. I don't need to get distracted by a set of pretty eyes.

What about a set of pretty legs?

"Again, no one asked your opinion. She probably doesn't even remember who I am." I make my way to the sitting area of my rooms and look out the window that faces the dense forest behind the building.

We could go for a quick run.

Memories of running through the forest on four paws, the scent of fresh dew on pine needles wafting through my nostrils, fill my thoughts.

"No. We can run after the meeting." I sit and pull the travel coffee cup stamped with "have a Tea-rific day with Enchantea" and take a deep swig. The coffee's rich house blend was the perfect pick-me-up I need, especially with how sweet the scones likely were, and I am not usually a sweet person. But for this meeting, I'll deal with it.

Opening my portfolio, I scan for the specifics I want to

review with Mr. Rogers. I had gone over it with Daisy a dozen times before flying out, but Rogers' reputation is not one to mess with. I need this deal to go through. The clan needs it. I take another swig of the coffee. The strong black brew has a subtle undertone of caramel and I make a mental note to order a bag as a gift for Daisy.

I didn't have time to think about scones, or the girl. I need to prep for this meeting.

My name, scrawled in what can only be Netti's neat hand-writing, catches my eyes. Her magic is tangible as I run a thumb over the looping letters. I sniff the box, her scent lingering on the cardboard is barely detectable over the sweets inside, and my skin prickles as though I've touched a live wire.

"It must just be the magic," I say before snapping the ribbon off the box and opening the lid, reveling in the delicate yellow scones piped with swirls of icing and nestled in the box with candied blueberries.

Picking up a scone, I sniff again, but nothing seems enchanted about them beyond the charming witch who made them. I take a bite, relishing the way the pastry melts like butter on my tongue with bursts of citrus and vanilla. The taste reminds me of lazy summer days under the sun, cozy naps by the fire, and the way my body seemed to vibrate when I touched her skin.

Netti.

Suddenly, my thoughts are consumed with her. My finger-tips burn where they brushed her collarbone, leaving a tingling sensation that lingers. The vanilla chai scent that wafted from her as she gracefully moved about the kitchen last night is as vibrant as though she were in the room with me. I find myself mesmerized by the memory of the way the strands of her hair, falling from her bun, delicately framed her face, accentuating her natural beauty.

As I sit at the table, an overwhelming restlessness builds within me, causing my body to feel constricted, as if my skin is too tight. What is happening to me?

Unable to contain this surge of energy, I push up from the table in a sudden motion, unintentionally scattering my papers and knocking over my coffee, the dark liquid spilling onto the cream-colored carpet. At that moment, though the mess seems inconsequential, my focus is solely on the burning sensation under my skin, reminiscent of the first time I ever transformed into my wolf form. The intensity of my emotions and physical sensations is undeniable, leaving me desperate to uncover the reason behind this inexplicable connection to her.

I shake my head, trying to clear my thoughts, but all I can think about is her.

Wolf?

...

Silence.

...

This is not good.

CHAPTER 3
NETTI

I stand sleepy-eyed in front of the kitchen sink, feeling out of sorts. My roommate, Alita, had already come and gone before I had dragged myself out of bed. After cleaning up my mess and baking the scones, I forced myself to stay up, even as my eyelids drooped heavily, to work on my essay. Throughout the night, I had been plagued by dreams of that shifter.

Even now, I still feel the phantom touch across my collarbone, as though he had marked me. But that wasn't possible, was it?

Growing up in a household full of witches who ran a bookshop, I had seen my fair share of shifters, vampires, and other creatures of lore. The moment he stepped through the door, I immediately pinned him for a shifter. From the way he walked, his predatory grin, and the otherworldly glint in his blue eyes, I would bet he belonged to one of the wolf clans. I had never been with a wolf shifter before, but I had heard the rumors and wouldn't need to be asked twice.

Shaking my head, I pull my hair into a messy bun and start washing the dishes I was too tired to finish the night before.

He was a stranger from out of town. Not only that, but he probably forgot me the moment he stepped out of the door.

I had too many things on my plate between college, the bakery, and family to even think about dating. Especially not some rich stranger who I only met once—who probably had dozens of women vying for his attention.

Despite Connor Abernathy's undeniable handsomeness, it was not the only thing that mattered. In fact, his looks were more than enough to make anyone weak in the knees. After submitting my assignment with two minutes to spare before midnight, I couldn't help but dive into a Google search about what Mr. Hotshot Bossy Grumpypants did for a living. As the search results popped up on my screen, I was greeted with numerous images of him engaging with mayors, cutting ribbons in front of impressive buildings, and attending glamorous galas with stunning women dressed in outfits that would cost me more than my monthly salary.

With a sigh, I refill the coffee maker and set a single cup to brew. Meanwhile, I start making a list of things I have to do before I start my shift at 1:00 today. It's a necessity for me. Without my daily list, I would be lucky if I didn't forget my own tasks. Sometimes, I even half-joke about making a memory pastry to eat with breakfast, so that I don't forget anything. I pick up my cup, relishing in the warmth against my fingertips.

The scones.

The shattering of porcelain echoes against the linoleum, followed by shrieks from Honey, who swoops in and lands on my head. I curse as I step backward to avoid the shards of my favorite coffee cup and spilled coffee.

I forgot to tell Connor he had to concentrate on what he wanted to focus on.

Fishing for my phone out of my purse, I wedge it between my cheek and shoulder as I grab the broom and sweep the broken cup together in a pile. The phone rings before Alita cheerfully picks it up.

"Magickal Morsels bakery where every day is a magickal day, how can I hel–"

"Alita, it's Netti," I say in a rush, tapping my foot and leaning on the broom. "Has the customer Connor picked up his order yet? The ones with the focus scones from last night."

"Well, good morning to you too, sleepyhead. Did you get a good rest?" Alita muffles the receiver on the other end as she calls out, "Have a good day!"

"Alita!" I hiss, storming off into the hall to find the dustpan. "This is important!"

"Yes, yes. Don't get your panties in a twist. He picked them up bright and early this morning. Grumpy but quite scrumptious. I could eat a man like him up without being asked twice." She whistles. "Did you get his number?"

I let out a groan, letting my body sag against the wall as I pull my knees to my chest.

"Oh, don't be down, Netti. I'm sure one bite of your baking, and he will be back begging for more."

"That's not the issue. He came in for an order of focus scones–"

"And you gave him a love spell," she gasps, but I can hear the joking undertone in her voice.

"No!" I whisper over the receiver, as if someone will overhear me alone in our condo. "You know love spells are illegal, let alone rarely work."

"Then, what is it? Some of us are trying to work here." Pots and pans clang together in the background.

"Well... I made the scones, as usual, and told him when to eat them and how long they'd last. The problem is, I forgot to tell him the most important thing: to be thinking about what he wanted to focus on when he ate them."

"Oh boo, so you might have made him concentrate on his next trip to his private island instead of this meeting. I'm sure it'll be fine; he seemed so uptight. If he's not thinking about the meeting, then a vacation will do him some good."

I groan, my temples beginning to throb. I rub at them with my fingers, hoping to ease the pain.

"What if he comes in and complains?"

"Then, you flash him that sunshine smile of yours, get his number, and give him something positive to focus on besides work. Now, get yourself cleaned up. It's a madhouse, and I've got to run to pick up some packages from the post office on my break after you clock in." The phone clicks and goes dead.

Of course, that's the advice she would give.

I quickly clean up my mess, the sound of clattering dishes blending with the gentle hum of the heater, and make a new cup of coffee in my glittery aluminum travel mug. The unicorn rearing on the side proclaims, *"Sparkle like no one is watching. There is magic inside you."*

I add an extra dollop of caramel sauce and heavy cream, the sweet smell lifting my spirits before I screw on the lid.

I can do this.

I run to the bathroom, pulling on my favorite pastel pink dress and swiping on some mascara and lip gloss before grabbing my bag. Honey squeaks from his perch in the corner of the room where he's hanging upside down, wings tucked in tight. I scratch the top of his head and blow him a kiss.

"You can't come today. I'm not working the closing shift. Don't cause any mischief while I'm gone," I whisper, wagging a finger at him as I grab a plate of banana slices from the fridge before throwing my phone, keys, and wallet into my purse.

The chilly morning air bites at my cheeks as I walk down the sidewalk, only to remember my still-steaming coffee and lunch back at home.

I would not starve working in the bakery, but I am saving every penny I can, so packing my lunch instead of going out adds up. The tantalizing aroma of freshly baked bread and pastries is a hard temptation to resist, but most days, I hold my resolve. That and there was no way I would survive today without caffeine and sugar. I rush back to the door, my hurried footsteps echoing in the empty street. Fumbling with my keys until I find the right one, I insert it into the lock and jog inside. Tucking my lunch bag under my arm, I run outside, and close the door. I struggle to maintain my balance as I juggle the keys. Suddenly, my coffee tips to the side, the scalding hot liquid cascading down my arm and over my skirt.

"Shit," I yelp, the searing pain making me jump back. The burning sensation lingers, a reminder of my carelessness. Instinctively, I stick out my arms to avoid getting the coffee anywhere else. I didn't have time for this, but I couldn't show up to work covered in a sticky mess. Determined, I hastily wash up and change, sighing as the cool water soothes my scalded skin. Finally, I grab all my things and check twice before locking the door and heading toward the bakery.

I glance down at the watch on my wrist before turning the corner toward Main Street at a brisk walk. After all my delays, I only have twenty minutes until the start of my shift and the bakery is a fifteen minute' walk away if I take the shortcut. My eyes glance longingly toward the deep green of the forest dotted with burnished golds and reds. I have always loved nature, so finding a condo that faced the woods was the sign I needed when I came to tour Rusthollow when I was trying to leave home.

"You don't have time to go the long route today," I tell myself out loud as I glance longingly at the winding dirt path.

Inhaling the crisp late autumn air, I let the smell of ever-greens mingling with wood smoke rejuvenate me. That is, until the scent brings back the memory from last night of the handsome shifter leaning over the counter. Heat creeps into my cheeks, and I brush the thought away. Just as Alita said: we'd probably never see him again.

I turn left, away from the forest, cutting through the neighborhood that would lead me directly to the heart of town.

"Good morning, Mrs. Taylor!" I wave at the elderly witch pulling weeds in her immaculate front yard as I reach the row of Victorian-style homes.

"Good morning, Netti. Off to the bakery?" She sits back on her haunches and lifts her gaze to meet mine, the sun dancing along her tanned face. The corners of her eyes crinkle as she lifts a hand in greeting.

"Yes, I've picked up an extra shift today." I glance at my watch, not wanting to be rude but I don't have time to stay and chat.

"It's exhausting seeing you constantly running from school to work and back again. You're a young witch. You should live a little."

"You know what they say, Mrs. Taylor: Work hard, play hard." I plaster a fake smile on my lips.

"You're not fooling me, girl." She shoves her spade into the flower bed beside her, where the fall chrysanthemums are bursting in warm shades of orange, red, and yellow. "I've lived a long life, and you have a bright aura, but I can see it wearing on you."

"It's just this time of year. End-of-the-semester projects and all. I promise once winter brea—"

"That is peculiar." She leans over her white picket fence and I turn around, but nothing is amiss—just another row of houses.

"What is it?"

She lifts a hand and gestures around me. "There is something different about you today. More than just you overworking yourself. Have you met someone new recently?" Her hazel green eyes meet mine, and my palms begin to sweat, my stomach tying up in knots.

Could she possibly know about the stranger from last night?

"I meet lots of strangers all the time working in the bakery," I stammer, but I feel the pull of her magic and swear even the flowers in her garden turn to look at me.

"I know you don't have time this morning to come in for tea, but can I see your palm?" She raises a graying eyebrow and holds out her hands.

"Umm, sure." I bite my bottom lip and switch my mug to my right hand to offer her my dominant hand. Her lips press together in a firm line before she grabs my wrist, her cool finger tightening around the skin and opening my palm. She makes little humming noises as she traces the lines.

Mom once told me one of my great aunts had read tea leaves and palms. She had always scoffed at the notion that your future was set in skin, but she'd never left an empty tea cup's dregs alone.

Minutes tick by as I wait impatiently, my heartbeat thudding in my ears, for her to tell me some story that I'm working too hard, or my career choice is a poor one and I should have stayed at home and been the ugly duckling of magic in the family. While the boss would be understanding, the thought of being late turns my stomach sour, adding to the tight knot of tension that has taken residence this morning.

"Netti." Her voice snaps me out of my spiraling thoughts, but her eyes look faraway as though she was seeing through me. "You have run into your life mate, but something is blocking the bond. Catch him before the next full moon, or else your life will take a turn down a dangerous path."

"What do you mean, my life mate?" My brows furrow together. There was no way she could mean the guy from last night.

She drops my hand as a car passes behind us, breaking the moment.

"Best you get to work. These old bones need rest." She pats me on the arm before turning around and making her way up the path to her front door.

She couldn't be right. There was no way I was mated to a shifter, let alone a billionaire. Right?

CHAPTER 4
CONNOR

The harsh sunlight glares angrily through the dusty windshield, casting sharp rays of light into the car as I pull into the crowded parking spot in front of the bustling coffee shop that's only a few minutes walk from Rogers' office. The hum of car engines and the distant chatter of people fill the air, creating a cacophony of sounds that pierce through the quiet morning of the small town.

The rich aroma of freshly brewed coffee wafts through the open car window. Cool metal brushes against my fingertips as I reach into my pocket to retrieve my phone. The LED screen illuminates a bright glow, confirming I am fifteen minutes early for the meeting. The anticipation weighs heavily on my shoulders, causing a knot to form in my stomach.

This deal going through would greatly impact my pack, my family—even if they don't know it.

With a deep breath, I straighten the gold moon-shaped cufflink on my shirt sleeve, its intricate design reminiscent of my pack's emblem. I glimpse my reflection in the rearview mirror, remembering the same golden hue of the small hoops that were adorning *her* delicate earlobes.

A surge of heat rushes through my body, making my skin tingle and my senses heighten. The urge to embrace my inner wolf—to rip the skin from my bones and lose myself in the primal instincts—becomes almost overwhelming. In a fit of frustration and pent-up energy, I slam my fist against the hard edge of the steering wheel, the impact reverberating through the car and momentarily drowning out the surrounding sounds.

Maybe you should take out some of that pent-up frustration with a certain pink-haired witch.

"Where have you been?" I growl.

You turned down my offer to go for a run.

"You've been throwing a temper tantrum?" My brows furrow as I grab my wallet and open the car door.

When was the last time you let loose your control and just had fun? I bet that ray of sunshine could teach you a thing or two.

"I don't have *time* for fun. You know we have responsibilities. The clan comes first."

The clan you left instead of claiming your rightful place as alpha?

"That's not what happened, and you know it. I don't have time for this." I slam the car door shut and press the lock on the digital keypad. "Plus, she did something to those scones. They were supposed to help me focus, to ensure this meeting goes perfectly. We can't afford one misstep or to lose this deal. But I can't seem to concentrate on it or anything else."

Except her.

I grunt in response, pushing open the door to EnchanTea for the second time today.

"Mr. Abernathy. Welcome back. Was there something

wrong with your coffee this morning?" The barista calls from behind the counter. The air was still and quiet in the nearly empty coffee shop, except for the occasional murmur of the lone patron—a tall, lithe man in black who sat in the back corner sipping his coffee.

Vampire.

I feel the rumble of a growl from deep in my chest, but I shake my head at my inner wolf before I proceed further.

"No, just back for a fresh cup before my meeting," I reply, but a flash of pink catches my eye. I whip around, but it's only a small child holding a pink balloon bouncing behind her, clutching the hand of her mother.

"Is everything okay? Do you want a decaf?" she asks, pausing as she holds out the paper travel cup in her hands, pen poised and ready to scrawl my name. As I observe her handwriting, so different from Netti's looping scrawl on the box of scones, I can't help but wonder what that witch has done to me. Even women I've dated have not been on my mind as much as she has. I shake off the thought and respond, "No, just a house black to the brim, please."

"You've got it," she says, turning around to fill the paper cup with coffee. As she works, she continues the conversation, asking, "How's your time in Rusthollow been so far?"

"Fine," I reply, keeping my response brief.

"Have you been to Magickal Morsels yet? They make the most delicious pastries," she suggests. "In fact, some of our goods in the glass display are from them."

"Yes, I have, and no, I do not want any," I answer curtly, not interested in adding another baked treat to complicate my day.

"Is there anything else I can get you, then?" She smiles brightly at me, her short, curly blonde hair bouncing around her face.

"No. Just the coffee." I glance down at my watch and tap

my foot. My veins throb with the intense heat, a fiery torrent that makes my skin feel like it's about to burst. I can hardly take it anymore. I need to leave this building and find some fresh air. "I need to leave. I have a meeting."

"Oh well, have a good day then!" she says cheerfully, placing a lid on the cup and handing it to me. I lay the bill on the counter, take the hot cup from her hands, nod, and leave the cafe.

The heat radiating from the coffee is nearly scalding as I gulp down a mouthful, but I need something—anything— to clear my head. Until the lingering flavor of French vanilla buttercream hits my tongue, and I groan. Had I had less restraint over my wolf, I would have tasted more than frosting last night.

"No, this can't be." I rip off the lid and peer down at the inky black surface. Perfectly normal house roast, no cream or sugar, just how I like it. Then, why was the taste of frosting so intense?

I take another sip. Normal. Not a hint of vanilla.

Maybe Daisy was right. After this deal went through, I'd find some time for myself.

As I approach the building, the sunlight reflects off the mirrored windows, creating a dazzling display. The sleek, white facade of the office building exudes a sense of modernity and professionalism. A quality I both respect and utilize in my architectural designs. The copper sign near the front door catches my eye, adding a touch of elegance to the overall design bearing the logo of Summit Contracting Group. The sounds of traffic and city life buzz behind me, blending into a familiar urban symphony. The town of Rusthollow may be quaint, but in the short time I've been here, the atmosphere has been addicting.

"It's now or never." I crush the last of the coffee, but before I take a step, a bat swoops before me.

"Sorry! The bats get a little brave this time of year. Mr. Abernathy?" A plump, middle-aged woman waves from the tall glass door, her brown hair pulled into a bun at the top of her head.

"Yes, it is quite unusual. Trash?" I lift my empty cup.

"Oh, here, let me take that. Mr. Rogers is particular about recycling." She holds open the door with one hand and gestures for the empty cup with the other. "I'm Mrs. Willows, his assistant. If you'll just follow me."

I store that bit of information, as it could come in handy later. Abernathy Incorporated kept up pretty standard recycling standards, but policies could be updated to be more proficient if it meant a partnership.

I follow her through widely spaced hallways covered in large abstract paintings, sunlight filling the room from the sunroof window tiles, giving the place an overall cheerful, cozy atmosphere.

"Does Mr. Rogers work remotely from here all the time?" I ask as we turn to the left and up a flight of stairs.

"Recently, he's been working more from here. Since his wife passed, this was their favorite office to come visit."

"I'm so sorry to hear that."

"Life is fleeting. You must take charge of it while it's fresh in your hands." A tall gentleman with salt and pepper hair steps from the office at the end of the hall and opens his arms wide in greeting. "You must be the infamous Connor Abernathy. Taking the industry by storm."

"Yes, sir. I am incredibly grateful for your acceptance of my invitation to discuss this proposal in person. I'm looking forward to our meeting." I extend my hand toward him. He grips it firmly, giving a small shake.

"You've made quite a name for yourself in a short period of time, Mr. Abernathy. I'm not usually impressed by much being in the industry as long as I have, but you are a rarity. Come, let's discuss this further," he says as he gestures to his office. "Trish, could you get me a vanilla chai latte please? Abernathy, would you like anything?"

"Just water, please." I nod before following him.

He gestures toward a wide table, situated in front of a wall of floor-to-ceiling windows offering a breathtaking view of a lush plot of pines and maples that stretch out behind his office.

"Have you ever lived out in a small town, Abernathy?" he says, sitting on the chair at the head of the table and swiveling to face outside.

"Growing up, but not for a long time. I've mostly stayed in Port Nicholes for the last few decades." I sit at the table and place my folder and notepad on the polished wood surface.

"That's too bad." He drums his fingers on the table.

"Why's that, sir?" I'm anxious to discuss the proposal to unite our companies on this project.

"There is something... magical about towns like these. You really get to feel your inner nature." He turns and stares directly at me with his solemn brown eyes, and the knot in my stomach tightens. Was he talking about my wolf?

"Here you go," Mrs. Willows says, her gentle voice reaching my ears as she places a cool glass of water on a coaster before me and a cup before him. The aroma of the steaming vanilla chai wafts toward me, enveloping my senses and causing my nostrils to tingle, reminding me of the scent of... her. Thoughts of Netti consume my mind, her presence lingering in the air like a sweet and alluring fragrance. My body reacts, a subtle tightening in my trousers, as I imagine her curves beneath her apron, my fingers tracing every inch of her silky smooth skin.

Suddenly, a warm hand lands on my shoulder, jolting me back to reality. I flinch away, momentarily startled. "I'm so sorry. Jet lag," I stammer, my mind still lost in the depths of desire. What was going on with me? I glance weakly between Mrs. Willows and Mr. Rogers, attempting to regain my composure.

"You look a little peckish," Mrs. Willows remarks, her voice filled with concern. "Are you sure there isn't anything I can get you?"

"No, thank you," I reply, my throat feeling parched like a desert. I reach for the glass of water, its coolness soothing against my fingertips. I take a sip, feeling the dryness dissipate, but the heat still lingers, an unspoken tension in the air. The urgency builds within me, the need to escape, to run, as if we are engulfed in flames.

Can't you feel the magic, the raw energy coursing through our veins?

Ignoring my inner wolf, I gulp down half the glass of water, desperate to quench the burning sensation within. I meet Mr. Rogers' gaze; his disappointment is evident in the pursed frown upon his lips.

"Have you traveled much?" He raises an eyebrow quizzically at me.

"I have. Although never to Rusthollow." I use a finger to loosen the collar around my neck. "I had some pastries at the bakery down the street from where I'm staying. They must not be settling."

"At Magickal Morsels? Their baked goods are to die for. Not to mention, they employ the most cheerful bakers I've ever met. My Chloe loved to visit them any chance she got." A wistful look crosses his face, but is gone as soon as it comes.

Suddenly, I'm overwhelmed by the lingering scent of her, the ghost of her touch on my fingertips, and the burning ache in my chest. I shift uncomfortably in my seat, feeling the soft cushion beneath me. "Yes, they had quite the variety," I reply, opening my notebook and turning to the first page. The sound of the pages rustling mixes with the low hum of conversation down the hall in the background. "As the CEO of Aber--"

"A lone wolf," he interrupts, sipping from his cup. I can hear the delicate clinking of the porcelain against his lips. He observes me intently, and I feel like a pup caught sneaking out past curfew, the weight of his gaze pressing on me.

"Yes?" My ears start buzzing and all I can hear above it is the memory of her repeating my name when she took my order. I finish the rest of my water and straighten out my cuffs. "I do have a team that works with me, but I like to make meetings like this more personable."

He strums his fingers together and leans over the table. "A quality we share, but that's not what I was referring to. Why did you leave your pack?"

"Excuse me?" His question momentarily stuns me. I knew Rogers was very particular about who he worked with, but I wasn't expecting him to bring up that past. Pack business stays in the pack.

"Clearly, you're alpha material," he continues, gesturing to me. "I've been watching your company—you—over the years. Watching how you navigate. You've got a smart head, but an alpha never leaves their pack behind. So tell me, why did you leave?"

Sweat beads along the back of my neck. Why I left wasn't a secret, or cowardice. Twin wolves born to the pack leader both developing Alpha traits. We would have been at each other's throats, neither of us backing down. I didn't want the pack to tear in two, and I wasn't kneeling so I did what I thought was best. I left.

I always left. I never made attachments. That's why I

couldn't understand why I couldn't get the witch out of my head. She had to have done something. Was she secretly working for a rival company, trying to sabotage this meeting? I have to know. I have to confront her.

As the thoughts race through my mind, my heart pounds against my chest, a physical manifestation of my growing anger and frustration. The adrenaline surges through my veins, causing a tingling sensation that spreads from my fingertips to my toes. My muscles tense, ready for action, as a surge of energy courses through my body.

With each passing second, my breathing becomes shallow and rapid. The air feels heavy, as if I were suffocating under the weight of my emotions. Sweat begins to bead on my forehead, trickling down my temples as my body's temperature rises in response to the intensity of my anger and the desire I was burning up for her.

"Do you have a bathroom I can use?" I push up from the table, pulling out a napkin to dab at my forehead. "The scones..."

"Yes, down the hall and take a right before the stairs." He leans back in his chair and crosses his arms over his chest.

I turn and book it down the hall as professionally as I can manage. This was not going according to plan, and it was all her fault. I never should have tempted fate and just relied on myself. Pushing past the bathroom doors, I move to the sink and splash my face with water, trying to cool down the burning sensation inside me.

"Fuck!" The fear, like icy tendrils, coils around my stomach, causing it to churn and knot. My hands tremble involuntarily, betraying the anxiety that consumed me. Yes, I could go with another company, but it would mean greater costs, an extended timeline, and products of a lesser quality. There was a reason I was going to such lengths to secure Summit

Contracting Group. My pack and my company deserved no less. Even if they were clueless about where the support was coming from.

Emotions have a profound impact on the body, influencing our physiology in ways both subtle and overt. The surge of anger, fear, and determination I'm experiencing are like a storm raging within me, affecting my heart rate, breathing pattern, muscle tension, and even my facial expressions. I need to cool down before I face Rogers and try to pull this all back together. Then, I will deal with the witch.

What if she wasn't doing it on purpose?

"How would you know that?" I growl, straightening out my tie and tugging at my cuffs.

Do you remember how tired she looked? The faint dark circles under her eyes.

Guilt coils in my gut as the image of her flashes in my head, followed by the strong urge to protect her.

"It doesn't matter. She needs to give me a counterspell, but first I need to fix this."

Inhaling deeply, I open the bathroom door and am startled to find Mrs. Willows standing, holding my notepad and folder, and looking anxious.

"I'm sorry, but Mr. Rogers had to step out for the rest of the evening. He said he'd be in touch about rescheduling."

Fuck!

CHAPTER 5
NETTI

"Netti! Just the person I was hoping to grab." Hazel's voice comes through the phone. "I have a huge favor to ask."

My stomach drops, and I rub my eyebrows, glancing around at the patrons eating their pastries before turning away.

"Is it little Eddie again?"

"Yes," she groans, and I can hear clattering on the other end of the receiver. "You know what it's like... well, you don't but he's sick again. I need to run him to the doctor's to see if it's another ear infection. Otherwise, no one is going to get any sleep tonight."

"Poor thing. I hope he gets better soon." I hold my breath while waiting for the request I know is coming.

"Is there any way you could cover my closing shift tonight? I don't think I can come in. Eddie, put that down right now!" A loud thunk followed by crying echoes in the background. It wasn't the first time I'd covered for Hazel when she couldn't make it in because her toddler was getting sick since the weather had started getting colder.

"Of course, Hazel. Let me know if there is anything you need." I smile, hoping it comes through the receiver. I was the oldest of four kids. I remember how every cold season went with little ones.

I hang up the phone with a sigh and wipe my hand on my apron. At least it was Thursday.

As the hours drag by, I diligently finish going through the extensive list of inventory items, meticulously checking off each item as I go. With a sense of accomplishment, I pick up the phone and call the grocer, placing our order for tomorrow. Surprisingly, there were no special or urgent orders needing to be prepped for Friday, which is a rare occurrence. Thankfully, our standard stock for EnchanTea seemed sufficient to meet the demand. As I take a moment to look up from my task, I notice that the once bustling shop is now completely empty, and the usually busy street outside is unusually quiet. Despite the stillness, a gentle smile forms on my face, knowing everything is in order and ready for the next day of business.

I might have time to finish prepping the orders before closing time and leave a little early. I'd been dying to swing by the used bookstore, but they ware always closed before I finish my shift, and I'd rarely had time to wander into town.

Did I even have time to read books?

With a sigh, I grab a rag and start cleaning off the tables. I was so tired lately I couldn't even remember to tell a customer the most important instructions for his order.

"Oh shoot, someone needs to feed Honey!" I dash to my purse and pull out my cell phone. With a sense of urgency, I hit the speed dial for my roommate's number.

"Hey, Netti. Are you off work yet?" she asks, and I hear the sound of people laughing on the TV in the background.

"Yes, but Hazel called out. Eddie's sick again," I reply. I shift uneasily on my feet, then sink into a nearby chair, sighing with relief as I pull the tie out of my bun. As I let my hair fall around my shoulders, the weight of the week's tension seems to ease, a brief reprieve from the stress. A gnawing frustration keeps me from feeling content, and it's more than just Hazel asking me to stay late for her.

"Again?" she responds, her voice filled with disbelief. "Let me guess, you said you'd cover for her?"

"Mhmm, yes," I reply, twisting the phone cord around my finger. The bakery was the only place I knew who still used a corded phone. Even my parents upgraded our house and shop to have wireless phones.

"You're such a softie." She laughs.

"She needed the coverage, and I need the money," I explain, my thoughts drifting to the upcoming bills. It's not just the condo expenses but also the costs for my final semester in the nursing program. On top of that, Honey, my fruit bat, recently got injured, and the vet bill has put me even further behind financially than I had anticipated.

"I don't understand why you don't apply for some grants or scholarships," she suggests, her voice trailing off.

"I just..." My gut tightens, and I stare at the waning moon outside the window.

"I get it. It's a sense of proprietorship, but Netti, it's literally free money they're giving to help you learn. You deserve it."

The bell above the door jingles, and I jump from the chair.

"Welcome to— Alita, I'm going to have to go." My eyes flick to the shifter who shut the door behind him. He looks worse for wear, hair mussed and eyes cold as he stares at me hungrily.

"You okay?" she asks, worry lacing her tone.

"Yep, I'm fine. Just customers. I'll see you when I get home," I quickly reply before ending the call and dropping my phone into my pocket. "Connor," I say breathlessly, and I can't help but notice how his muscles bulge against his black button-up shirt.

"Witch, what have you done to me?" He stares at me with eyes nearly feral. I step back, my pulse racing as adrenaline floods my system—prey before a predator.

"Wh-what are you talking about?" I twist the edge of my apron in my hands, glancing between him and the front door. Would running from a shifter only urge their hunt instincts? It wasn't the full moon; it was still a few days from now. What was going on?

"You. This." He steps toward me, eyes leaving burning trails along my body as he examines me head to toe. "The scones."

Oh no. The scones.

"I'm so sorry," I stammer and take another step back, the counter bumping against the back of my legs.

"You're sorry?" He places a hand on either side of me on the counter, pinning me in. The smell of wood and cinnamon fills the space between us as heat radiates from his body. Conflicting emotions rise in me; I should want to run, but heat coils in my guts and I don't feel afraid. "You could very well have cost me and my company," he growls. "Your scones made me do anything but focus."

"Wh-what are you talking about?" I focus on the buttons of his shirt but dread pools in my gut. I can't control my magic and now I am losing touch with making potions and pastries? I close my eyes tightly, walking through the memory of making the pastries that night. I followed the recipe exactly as I always did, but I was tired that night.

Oh Netti, what did I do?

"I still can't think of anything *except you*." Connor's voice is a low rumble and drags me from my spiraling thoughts. He leans forward, and the stubble of his beard scratches the delicate skin of my neck. Heat coils in my gut and all I can think about is giving in for once until he pulls back and grabs me by the chin, forcing me to meet his gaze.

"Wait, me?" My eyebrows pinch together in confusion. What did the scones have anything to do with me?

"Make it stop," he demands.

"Make what stop?" I shake my head to clear my hazy thoughts.

"Whatever you've done to me. Make it stop. Give me a counterspell." He moves closer until I feel the warmth of his breath on my skin.

"The magic in the scones?" I laugh at the absurdity.

"Yes, witchling. Remove this sorcery you've placed on me."

"I've placed no such spell on you," I protest. Pushing against his chest, I am met with firm resistance.

"Lies, I have not been able to think of anything but you since I ate those scones this morning," he whispers, tightening his grip. His eyes glance to my lips and I have to swallow the lump in my throat. "If that's not a love spell..."

"Love spells are illegal," I snap, trying to pull from his grasp. How dare he accuse me of giving him a love spell? Not to mention, what would that gain me? I hardly even knew the man, let alone had the time to concoct some elaborate scheme, even if I knew how. I didn't need to trick someone by magic. "I forgot to tell you to think of your meeting or whatever you wanted to focus on when eating them. I tried to call the shop this morning, but you had already picked up your order and hadn't left any contact information."

"I was not thinking of you after I left," he denies. A muscle in his jaw twitches.

Seconds tick by in silence as we stare at each other alone in the bakery. "Well, whatever you were thinking of, the magic in those scones should only last two to three hours. They would have worn off hours ago."

As I try and fail again to extricate myself from his arms, I feel the rough texture of his fingertips against my skin, sending a shiver down my spine. I manage to move to the side, the coolness of the glass counter behind my back contrasting with the heat radiating from his body. The evidence of his thoughts presses firmly into my abdomen, sending a wave of desire coursing through me. A small gasp escapes my lips, mixing with the sweet scent of vanilla lingering in the air. Wetness pools between my legs, a physical response to the intensity of the moment.

"Netti," he growls before fisting his hand in my hair, tugging gently but firmly.

My senses are overwhelmed as he crushes his lips to mine, the taste of his lingering coffee on his breath. Another gasp escapes as my body betrays me, arching into him on its own accord. My hands pressing against his chest curl into the soft black silk of his button-up, the smoothness of the fabric adding to the sensory overload. We stumble backward, the clatter of metal cookie sheets on the counter resonating throughout the small kitchen.

He slams me against the pantry door, the solid wood providing a sense of security as we hide away from prying eyes that may wander into the bakery. "I've thought of nothing but you all day, little nettle." He runs his teeth along the bare column of my neck, sending shivers down my spine and eliciting a gasp that echoes in the intimate space.

"I. We." I can't catch my breath or my thoughts as his fingers move to my hip and knead into the delicate skin, his face buried against my neck. "Connor," I gasp as the intensity of desire and arousal floods through my body. I can feel its physical effects taking hold. A rush of heat spreads from the pit of my stomach, surging like a wildfire through my veins. Each breath becomes shallow and quick, as if my lungs are unable to capture enough air to satisfy the growing need within me.

He says he's under some spell, but what explains these feelings he elicits in me? I've never had good control over my magic, had I manifested a curse in my loneliness?

"Connor. Please." My thoughts become fragmented, scattered like puzzle pieces that refuse to fit together. The touch of his fingers on my hip sends electric sparks dancing across my skin, igniting a tingling sensation that travels up my spine. It's as if every nerve ending in my body is awakened, eagerly anticipating the next caress.

"Netti, I need you to release me," he demands, his voice a rumble against my skin. Heat flushes up my neck and into my cheeks. He presses his face against my neck, a delicious shiver racing down my spine, leaving a trail of goosebumps in its wake. The sensation is exhilarating and maddening, a sweet torment that leaves me longing for more. His touch becomes more intimate, fingers finding their way to my breast. Through the fabric, I can feel the teasing pressure, a delightful ache that sends waves of pleasure radiating from that sensitive point. The anticipation builds, causing my heart to pound faster, matching the rhythm of my racing thoughts.

When had I last let myself feel like this? When have I let myself allow a man to have this much effect over me? Never before had I felt such a dizzying, exhilarating rush, such utter surrender to another's influence. Also, when's the last time I gave in and enjoyed myself? I have no idea why this wolf shifter thinks I cursed him, but his very touch takes my ability to think clearly away. Maybe it's him who is enchanting me?

The phone begins to ring, and we spring apart, each

panting as we stare at each other, trying to catch our breath. Connor looks at me, then at the mess we've caused before returning his gaze to my swollen lips. He shakes his head as if trying to clear his thoughts before backing away.

"I need to go." He turns on his heels and leaves the cafe. I run to the phone, picking it up when I notice his warm knitted scarf on the ground. My cheeks heat as I stare at the discarded garment.

"Magickal Morsels Bakery, Netti speaking, how can I help you?"

"Netti, it's Rosemary! You weren't answering your cell, so I thought I'd try you at the bakery. I'm coming into town to visit you tomorrow! Surprise!"

CHAPTER 6
CONNOR

Cursing under my breath, I forcefully slam the bed and breakfast door shut, the sound reverberating through the air. I grimace, realizing that there might be other tenants in the neighboring rooms.

Ignoring the thought, I fixate on the sight of a half-eaten box of scones, its contents spilled and my name scrawled on the pristine white packaging.

Netti.

"Fuck." A surge of desire courses through me, my senses awakening at her memory. My dick stands at full attention as I recall how her hands tightened on my shirt as I pressed her against the bakery counter. I growl at my body's reaction to the mere thought of her.

We need her. My inner wolf whines.

"No, we don't." What I need is to get her out of my mind. She's said multiple times that she didn't spell the scones, but why else would she occupy my thoughts? She's gorgeous, but

I've known many beautiful women and none of them have had this effect on me.

Seeking solace, I make my way to the bathroom, forcefully yanking the shower curtain open. The hot water begins to flow, filling the compact space with swirling steam. In front of the mirror, I wipe away the condensation, revealing a smudge of her pink lip gloss on the side of my neck. My blood heats, and I tear myself away from the mirror, haunted by the image of her pinned against the wall, my face buried in her fragrant, soft pink hair as I drew moans from her lips.

She had responded with such intensity, as if she, too, were under some enchantment. Could someone have cursed us both?

"No, it can't be. That witch must have done something to me. But why? What would she gain from sabotaging the deal with Summit Contracting Group?" I muse out loud as I step into the steam-filled shower. The scalding water cascades over my body as I desperately scrub my skin, hoping to wash away the lingering memories that cling to me. But no matter how fiercely I scrub, I can't rid myself of the lingering sensation and fragrance of her presence. It's as if her essence has become intertwined with my own, haunting every breath I take.

Something in my chest tugs, and in my mind, I see her. Except she's not in the bakery but in a bed piled high with pillows and a quilted down comforter. Her hair is down, cascading over the pillows she's propped up against, reading a book.

"What witchery is this?" I growl, but my vision blurs until I can hardly see the shower around me. It's as though I'm in the room with her, except I'm not.

I feel a strum of excitement and arousal but it feels feminine and sweet as frosting.

In my mind's eye, Netti sets down her book, the cover

indiscernible, and looks around the room, her cheeks heating a warm pink. She's in nothing but a pink silk nightgown, clinging to her skin. Her nipples point against the thin fabric. I place one hand on the cold wall of the tile, the other reaching to grab around my thick shaft. The water continues to pelt against my skin, hot as sin. Its scorching heat envelopes my senses, yet my focus remains on Netti as she shifts in bed. Her legs part, and her hand ventures between her thighs.

"Fuck." A guttural growl escapes my lips as I tighten my grip. I don't know how it's possible, but I smell her, not just her sweet perfume, but the scent of her slick, intoxicating arousal.

With one finger gliding across her center, she uses her other hand to pinch her nipple. Her eyes close, her lips parted in a moan as her head drops back into the pillow. I mimic her movements, matching her stroke for stroke, wishing it was her delicate hands wrapped around my throbbing cock and my mouth exploring the depths between her legs. I growl again, clenching my teeth together, imagining her thighs tightening on either side of my head as I dip into her sweet tight center with one finger, then two, spreading her in preparation for my girth.

Oh, my sweet nettle, how I'd make you beg for your release.

Her hips buck up, her breathing increasing as though she heard my private thoughts. I feel the surge of her orgasm building, as though she's channeling her feelings directly into my head.

The words "Come for me" escape my lips in a barely audible guttural sound, accompanied by the rushing water from the showerhead. I concentrate on the vivid image of my head buried between her thighs, the sight of her glistening center, and the smell of her arousal filling the air. As I increase my pace, her eyes fly open, a moan escaping her lips, the sound echoing in the steam-filled bathroom. I can almost taste her pleasure as she reaches her climax, her body stilling in response. At that moment, it feels as if time stands still, and I swear I can see her silently mouthing my name, the sight of her lips forming the sound of "Connor."

I pant heavily, my muscles tightening with anticipation as I feel my release building. Leaning forward onto the shower wall, the cool tiles pressing against my skin, I grip onto the balls of my feet for support. The sensation of the water cascading down my body merges with the image in my mind, imagining her sweet lips wrapping around the head of my cock, the sensation of her warm breath against me. The intensity of the scene is enough to send me over the edge. My release comes on hard and fast, hitting the shower floor with a splatter, the sound of it mixing with the rushing water. The hot water quickly washes away any trace of my climax, leaving only the fading image of her in my mind.

As the image dissipates, I once again feel fully present in the shower, the sound of the water hitting the tiles and my heavy panting returning to the forefront of my senses. The scent of her arousal fades, replaced by the clean, soapy smell of the shower gel. I realize I have been completely lost in the moment, deeper than I had ever thought possible.

"That wasn't real. It's just the lingering effect of the scones," I say out loud, as though the proclamation would make it true. There is no way I could see into Netti's mind or her to push thoughts of herself into mine.

Was there?

To prevent myself from doing something I'll regret, I have to get away from her before I snap and fall prey to the magic, instinct, or whatever this was. I have to get out of this town. I didn't need a relationship to complicate things. Not now when I was trying to push for the biggest growth in my company's history. Not now when, if I can fix things with Summit

Contracting Group, it could mean hundreds if not thousands of people have more job and living opportunities.

"Good morning. How is small town life treating you?" Daisy's cheerful old voice through the car speakers is a balm to my scattered thoughts as I hit the answer button on the phone.

"Ready to come home."

Liar. You would like nothing more than to turn this car around and drive back to that bakery.

"How did the meeting go?" she says, the sound of a printer whirring in the background.

I open my mouth, but I can't bring myself to answer. I have hardly given the meeting a second thought, as hard as I tried. Everything I see or smell reminds me of her. Even sleeping the night before did nothing to quell the thoughts of Netti.

"That bad?" she says at my silence, her tone betraying a hundred other questions being held back.

"I'm driving back to the airport," I reply gruffly, watching the pines rolling past my window. It is a two-hour drive to the closest airport. I'd called as soon as I packed up after the shower to make sure my jet was ready for take-off as soon as possible.

"So soon? I thought I told you that you needed to take a break. You're going to work yourself to death," she chides.

More like die if I can't get my hands back on that pretty witch. You should have ripped that phone out of the wall or convinced her to close early and taken her back to the B&B. Then, you wouldn't have had to finish in the shower alone.

Now is not the time and place, wolf. And where have you been for the last twenty-four hours?

But my thoughts stray to my hand wrapped around my

cock as the hot water pounded against my skin, wishing it were her smooth hands--

"Connor?" Daisy's voice breaks my thoughts. I pinch the bridge of my nose with one hand as I slow the car down at the red light. I need to get a grip on myself.

"Sorry, I'm just trying to figure out how to clean up this mess." I sigh, pressing the gas pedal as the light flips green again. "We already discussed that I was flying home today. Plus, I have that board meeting Monday."

"The board meeting can wait. What happened?" she asks gently, like a mother. A sharp, icy ache settles in my chest, a silent reminder of my solitude.

It's more like what didn't happen. We didn't run through the forest, we didn't get the deal, and we didn't get the girl.

"Shut up," I growl.

"Excuse me?" Daisy says, and I can picture her peppered eyebrows shooting up into her hairline. Okay, make that two Christmas presents I'd need to order for her.

"Not you." I groan and sigh. "My wolf has been... acting strange lately. More talkative than usual."

"When was the last time you visited the pack? Or talked to your brother?"

The guilt I feel twists and churns in my stomach—a cold, heavy weight. I hadn't talked to my brother or the pack in over a decade since our last fight. Even though I constantly checked in on them, especially as I'd finished building projects or donated anonymously.

"What difference does it make?" I snap before biting my tongue.

Because wolves thrive in packs, and you are an alpha pretending to be a lone wolf.

"Connor, I know it's none of my business, but I've been around long enough to know you, and you care about the pack. Whether you will admit it or not," she says matter-of-factly. "You spend everything—your time, your money, your energy into their well-being—while your brother stands in as alpha and it's eating you. It doesn't surprise me at all that it's causing your wolf to act up."

Hey! I am not acting up...

"The pack needs it, and I help more than just my brother's pack. You know our goal at Abernathy inc. is to provide jobs and homes for all the magical and non-magical communities alike."

But at what cost to us?

"I know what you strive for, but I also see what it's doing to you. I'll see you Monday when you get back into the office. Drive safe." The line beeps and goes dead, the car switching back to the music channel.

I sit in brooding silence as I drive down the two-lane highway, the only sound being the faint hum of the engine. Towering pine and maple trees surround me, their branches reaching out like silent sentinels. The air inside the car feels stifling, my skin prickling with the heat as I tightly grip the steering wheel, trying to focus on my thoughts. But all I can see in my mind's eye is Netti's face, her half-smile and lifted surprised gaze from the bakery as I walked through the door. I can almost taste the plumpness of her lips after our passionate encounter.

"Fuck." Frustration boils like a red-hot poker inside me. I slam my fist against the steering wheel, the sound reverberating through the stillness. Rolling down the window, I hope for a refreshing breeze, but instead, a sweet vanilla chai scent fills my nostrils, a lingering reminder of Netti.

My phone buzzes, jolting me from my thoughts, and I glance down to see my brother's caller ID flashing on the screen. Confusion and curiosity flood my mind as I answer the call.

"Hello?" I say, my voice filled with a mix of apprehension and anticipation.

"Connor," my brother's voice crackles through the car speakers, the sound blending with the soft static of the radio. "I'm so glad I caught you."

"Carter." My twin, who I haven't talked to in goddess knows how long. My brother, who I conceded the pack to. What could he possibly want?

"You sound as cheerful as ever. Do you have any plans tonight?"

I do not have time for idle chit chat.

"I'm out of town. What do you want?" I growl my grip tightening on the wheel. I cannot face the pack or a confrontation with my brother right now. I need to get back home and figure out what to do now that summit contracting group's deal is a bust.

You need to turn around and find your witch.

"What a shame. I was wondering–"

The call drops and I glance down to see the bars on the screen of my cell have dropped to no signal.

"Well, so much for that," I sigh, but instead of relief my stomach turns. He probably thinks I purposefully hung up on him. Just another thing I've managed to fuck up this week.

The world seems to slow as I turn a corner, my eyes widening as I spot a deer standing in the middle of the road. Panic surges through me, my heart pounding as adrenaline courses through my veins. I stomp on the brakes, the screech of tires against pavement piercing the air. The car swerves uncontrollably, the tires losing traction as I desperately try to regain control. Finally, it spins off the road, hurtling toward a massive tree trunk.

In an instant, the impact sends shockwaves through my body, the airbags exploding into action, slamming me back into my seat. The smell of burnt rubber and smoke fills my nose as the seat belt digs into my shoulder, leaving a searing sensation. My ears ring, a constant buzz drowning out all other sounds. Time seems to stand still as I sit there, dazed and disoriented. Thoughts race through my mind, regret and uncertainty clouding my vision.

Maybe I should have stayed in town, sorted things out with Netti, and rescheduled the meeting with the Summit Contracting Group. Before I can fully process these thoughts, the world fades into darkness.

CHAPTER 7

NETTI

Peering at the letter from the bank, a heavy feeling settles in my stomach. I have picked it up at least two dozen times since I grabbed the mail this morning but haven't had the courage to open it yet. Instead of relaxing on my day off, I spent the morning and a significant portion of the afternoon completing a demanding essay, tackling a mountain of laundry, making a trip to the grocery store to stock up on supplies, and even managing to thoroughly scrub the bathroom, leaving it sparkling clean.

Anything to keep my mind off the bills...and him.

As if I needed any more complications in my life, I could not get the wolf shifter out of my mind.

Honey squeaks from his perch, stretching out his wings as he stares at me with his beady eyes.

"Fine," I sigh as I flip the letter over in my hand and grab my antique letter opener off my desk. "There is no point wallowing in misery. Best pull this bandaid off and deal with it."

I rip open the edge of the envelope, the sound of paper tearing echoing in the room, while silently praying to myself. As I pull the crisp white paper from its envelope, a faint scent of ink wafts up to my nose. Turning it over, my eyes are immediately drawn to the bold letters at the top.

DENIED.

Even though I've been anticipating it, the rush of disappointment washes over me like an icy wave crashing against my chest. I let the letter slip from my fingers, feeling the smooth texture of the paper as it slips through my grasp and gently flutters to the ground. Falling to my knees beside it,I grimace as the impact of the rough carpet bites at my legs through my thin jeans.

It isn't fair. Maybe this is a sign like grandmama's tarot cards.

The weight of the past two and a half years settles heavily on my shoulders, like a burden too heavy to bear. I had worked my ass off, the long nights and extra shifts etched into my exhausted bones. The countless sleepless nights and endless studying, all for this moment. And yet, here I am, denied my tuition loan in my very last semester.

As I try to make sense of it all, the sound of a familiar knock reverberates through the room, breaking through my thoughts. The door creaks open, and Rosemary's cheerful voice calls out, "Netti? I hope I have the right address. I'd hate to think I just magick'd my way into a stranger's home."

"I'm in here! Just cleaning up," I yell, quickly swiping up the mail to throw on my dresser to figure out later. Rosemary and I have been friends since grade school, our shared memories and laughter resonating in my mind. Even though we both left to study in colleges far away from our childhood home, we kept in touch. However, lately I've been so busy that I've been lacking on the communication.

I quickly wipe at my face and paste on a smile, hoping she can't see right through me.

"Netti!" She turns the corner, grabbing me in a bear hug and squeezes tight until I can hardly breathe.

"It's good to see you too, Rosemary." I stand back, my hands on her shoulders, and look from her auburn curls down to her freckled nose. "It looks like the sand and surf are treating you well."

"You know I can't tan to save my life. With this fair skin?" She scoffs as she pushes up her sleeves and shows off her freckled arms. "But I will say, the beach eye candy isn't bad." She tosses her bags to the floor and plops on the couch in our open-style kitchenette living room before toeing off her boots and patting the seat beside her. "You're a sight for sore eyes." I laugh as I take a seat beside her.

"So, what made you decide to take a trip to Rusthollow?" I gesture around me.

"Don't beat around the bush, Netti. Intuition. My witchy instincts are tingling." She peers at me with her wide hazel eyes, and it takes everything not to look away. She laughs and slaps me playfully on the arm. "Oh, your face. I'm just teasing you. You've just been quieter than usual, and you've declined all my invitations to come visit me, so I thought I'd take the opportunity to visit you. That is, if you haven't found someone to replace your best friend in the entire world."

"Rose—"

"You did!" She gasps in mock indignation. "Oh, who is it? Tell me more! Don't leave your girl hanging over the biggest life change since you kissed Matthew Hawks in eleventh grade. I have to know everything."

"This isn't high school, Rosemary. There isn't anyone—"

The words feel like a lie as heat infuses my cheeks and my thoughts stray to Connor's visit to the bakery. What was going on between us? I don't even know.

She looks at me skeptically, and my restraint in holding my tongue loosens. I was never good at keeping secrets around her. She always had a fifth intuition, even regarding small things like gifts and crushes. But I wasn't quite ready to open up about the encounter with Connor, even with her. And I trust Rosemary with my life.

"Well then, if there isn't anyone to tell me about, where can a girl get a good drink around here so you can update me on what's going on in Miss Netti Ellsworth's life?" she asks, her voice laced with anticipation. She links her arm with mine and tugs me off the plush couch.

"We could just stay in—" I start to suggest, but she cuts me off, her determination evident in the firm grip of her hand.

"I didn't just fly halfway across the country to stay in." She purses her lips, hands on her hips as she surveys me, her eyes scanning my face for any sign of resistance.

"I thought you flew in to see me?" I reply exasperatedly, a hint of mock hurt lacing my voice.

"Well yes, of course that is the main reason," she continues, her tone softening. "But it won't hurt to catch up while checking out where you've been holed up for the last three years." The weight of her words hangs in the air, a mix of nostalgia and curiosity.

"It's only been two and a half. You left half a year before me," I remind her, my voice tinged with playfulness.

"Two years, three years. The point is, we are well overdue for a girls' night out and a good drink and music," she declares, her eyes sparkling with excitement.

I ponder for a moment, thinking of the options. "Well, I've heard Taboos and Voodoos is highly recommended by some of the customers at the bakery," I offer, thinking of what else I'd overheard in conversation during work. "They're known for their wide selection of craft beers and signature cocktails."

A smile spreads across her face, her eyes lighting up with anticipation. "That sounds like a perfect plan. Let's go," she says, her voice filled with the promise of a memorable night as she tugs on my hand.

"I can't go looking like this," I sigh, running a hand over the soft fabric of my cable knit sweater. My jeans and sweater, usually comfortable and familiar, suddenly feel inadequate for the occasion. The thought conjures the image of Connor in his perfectly pressed dress shirt and slacks, the crispness of the fabric a stark contrast to the casual clothes I'm wearing. What would he think of my cozy, worn attire and messy life?

"You look fabulous. Very cozy-chic. It fits your sunshine personality, but right now, my little ray of sunshine is acting like a rain cloud. You need a cold drink, some friendly conver-sation, and maybe a hot body to loosen up all that tension." She winks as she pulls on her boots before grabbing her purse and heading out the door, leaving me no choice but to grab my purse and follow.

As we walk toward the club, I swipe my sweaty palms on my jeans and ignore my racing heart. Not even Rosemary is aware of my recent struggles, as I have kept them to myself. However, with her presence here, I realize how much I truly need her support and understanding. The comfort of confiding in her every night is something I deeply miss. Reluc-tantly, I even admit that I miss being home. Leaving was supposed to grant me a sense of freedom and purpose—a journey of self-discovery. However, as I approach the end of my degree, with only one semester left, I am beginning to question if I have taken on too much. Perhaps I am burning too many candles at once.

"Oh, look!" she exclaims, her eyes widening. "Let's grab a table in the corner." As she slides her arm through mine, I can feel the smoothness of her skin against mine and the spark of magic thrumming under her skin. With a gentle tug, she leads me across the polished wooden floor, its surface smooth and worn from years of dancing.

We arrive at a collection of round, dark wooden tables, their surfaces adorned with intricate carvings. I run my fingers along the edges, feeling the roughness beneath my touch. "Where would you like to sit?" I gesture around. We've arrived early, only a few other patrons slowly filtering past the bouncers.

"Here is fine." She smiles as she settles into a chair and then waves toward the bar.

I follow her gaze and am captivated by the dazzling display of shelves lined with rows of gleaming cut crystal decanters behind the old wooden bar. The bottles of wine, their labels adorned with vibrant colors, catch my eye, as do the mysterious potions swirling with an iridescent glow. Even in town, I'd never felt adventurous enough to go to a club, let alone one that catered to humans, witches, and other magical creatures.

"Chilton Bruha. What can I get you beautiful ladies?" A tall lanky man, with a blue-to-purple ombre faux hawk hairstyle, asks as he appears at the edge of our table, nearly startling me out of my seat. His dazzling smile, a flash of white teeth against tanned skin, is aimed at the two of us, but his hazel eyes linger on Rosemary, clearly appreciating how the fitted turtleneck and pencil skirt hug her curves. Who would blame him? Under the flashing lights from the dance floor, she could have been mistaken for a descendant of Aphrodite.

"The Sulky Selkies?" she asks, pointing to his faded grey band t-shirt and raising an eyebrow.

"It's the band playing tonight. Are you here to see them?"

"I can't say I've heard of them, but back in Oceanview, bands come and play nearly every night of the week. I know the owner. If they're interested in traveling, I could give her their contact."

"You didn't tell me you knew the owner of Luminous Lounge," I say, facing her in my seat.

"You didn't—"

"Well, now you know two club owners. How did you meet Marlena?" Chilton says, casually leaning against our table.

As she settles into a conversation with the owner of the club, I can't help but be drawn to the far corner of the room to the stage bathed in a deep red light. The sound of laughter and conversation fills the air, intermingling with the soft murmur of voices as more people filter into the club. As I strain my ears, I can hear the faint strumming of a guitar and the tapping of drumsticks as the band sets up, their instruments glinting under the crimson glow.

"Netti. Netti." Rosemary snaps her fingers in front of my face. I shake my head, turning to face her.

"Sorry, it's been a couple of long nights. What did you ask?"

"You're forgiven." She blows me a kiss. "What do you want to drink?"

"Drink? Oh--" My stomach drops as I think about the bill I found on the coffee table from the mail this morning. The bank's denial of my loan application meant I was facing the daunting prospect of finding another way to cover the remaining costs of my last semester. I had nearly forgotten until now. My budget was tight, and even the extra money I made from picking up shifts at the bakery wasn't enough to cover what I needed. "Just a water, please."

"We're out to have a good time," she says.

I glance around, taking in the vibrant scene before me. The air is filled with laughter and chatter, accompanied by the clinking of glasses and the soft music of the band starting to play in the background. The enticing aroma of various drinks wafted through the room.

"You can't drink just water," she insists, her voice tinged with playful defiance. I can see the determination in her eyes as she stares at me, challenging me to join in on the fun.

"I can drink just water. It's healthy," I reply, my voice carrying a hint of resignation. I shrug and break my gaze away, longing for the carefree abandon that seemed to surround us.

"If it's a matter of money—" she began, but before she can finish her sentence, my frustration gets the best of me.

"It's not money," I snap, instantly regretting my harsh tone. I meet her crestfallen features, realizing that my words had hurt her.

Thankfully, Chilton, the bar owner, intervenes at that moment. "Drinks are on the house tonight," he announces, his voice cutting through the tension. "We have a great selection of non-alcoholic cocktails if you prefer, but I cannot let you two go the night without a thank you after your friend here is connecting me with the owner of Luminous Lounge. You two are in my debt."

Relief washed over me, and I couldn't help but feel a tinge of regret for snapping at her. "Thank you," I said sincerely, my voice laced with gratitude. The weight of my earlier words begins to lift as I realize we were being taken care of, trying not to feel guilty over the free drink.

Feeling relieved, I decide to let go of my worries for tonight and focus on having a good time. Bills and homework can wait until tomorrow. "Can you make a French 75?" I ask Chilton, my curiosity piqued.

"Have you ever had a Fae 75?" he suggested, a mischievous smile playing on his lips. "It's a house special made with strawberry gin."

The description alone was enough to captivate me. "Well, I haven't, and that sounds fantastic," I reply, unable to contain my excitement. "We will take two. That is unless you want something different?"

"This week is about adventure and trying new things." Rosemary turns and looks at me, her eyes sparkling with enthusiasm. I couldn't help but smile back at her, feeling a warmth spread through me. Only a few moments later, we find ourselves sitting at our table, the glasses in front of us filled to the brim with the bubbling cocktail. The liquid swirls a delicate shade of baby pink, tempting us with its vibrant hue.

As I take a sip, the taste of summer strawberries dances on my tongue, sending waves of pleasure through my senses. It was as if I were lying under the stars, enveloped in the enchantment of the night.

"Wow, this is better than I ever could have imagined." I sigh contentedly.

"Did you ever imagine three years ago we'd be sipping Fae gin in a remote college town?" She laughs as she takes another sip.

"To be honest, I never thought I'd leave Willowdale." I stare at the bubbles popping at the top of my glass solemnly.

"What is it, Netti? You don't have to keep anything from me." Her warm hand clasps over my wrist, and I look up to meet her gaze. I feel my defense crumble as a glimmer of her magic runs along my skin.

"You don't need to use your magic on me," I say with a sigh before setting my drink on the table and closing my eyes.

"You know I can't help it. Sometimes it's intuition," she replies sheepishly. Rosemary's magic is heavily seeped in emotion. With just one touch, she can temporarily remove pain or boost happiness.

"I think I messed up big time." I pinch the bridge of my nose.

"Netti, what is it?" She pulls my hands away from my face and meets my gaze.

"I couldn't control my magic at home. I've barely managed to use it here. And now I think I've messed up a recipe for a customer that could have ruined his life. How can I ever be trusted to be a nurse?" Tears burn at the edge of my vision, and my throat feels as though it's closing tight.

"It can't be that bad, hun. And that's how you learn from your mistakes. Trust me, I've made loads of mistakes." She flicks her wrist toward the bar, and a stack of napkins flies to our table. I grab one and dab at my eyes, not even caring that my mascara has smeared, and I probably look like a trash panda. "Now tell me who broke your heart first, so I can beat them up."

"No one has broken my heart except me." Laughter bubbles up in my throat, punctuated by hiccups as tears stream down my face. "I'm on the edge of burnout. I'm working overtime every week on top of going to school, and I was just denied my loan for the last semester. I'll be dropped from the program if I can't come up with the money by the end of this semester."

"Have you tried asking your folks?" she asks, her voice filled with concern.

I shake my head, my heart heavy with disappointment. "They think moving out here wasn't a great plan. They wanted me to stay home and learn the family business," I reply with a sigh. "There is no way I can admit to them that I'm failing," I confess, the weight of failure settling on my shoulders like a suffocating blanket. The harsh fluorescent lights above the dance floor flash toward us, momentarily blinding me.

"Netti, you're not failing," she reassures me, her voice soft and comforting. I can feel her warmth radiating as she leans closer, her hand reaching out to touch my arm gently. The sensation of her touch sends a wave of relief through me, like a cool breeze on a sweltering summer day. "You've just hit a rough patch, but guess what? You're going to survive this, and you'll be stronger for it," she adds, her words filling the space around us with hope. "You've chased your dream, and I'm not going to let you give it up," she insists, determination resonating in her voice. "Now tell me about your tall, dark and handsome stranger," she prods, a mischievous twinkle in her eye. The clatter of a dropped glass shattering echoes in the background, followed by the crowd shouting huzzah as I hesitate, unsure of how to respond.

"How do you know he's—" I begin, only to be interrupted by her knowing smile. The sound of laughter drifts from a nearby table.

"It doesn't take a genius to see something affecting you more than school, work, and bills," she says, her words punctuated by the tinkling of her glass against the table. With a playful gesture, she reaches over the table and pinches my cheek, a fleeting touch that brings back memories. I swat her away, a mixture of annoyance and amusement coursing through me.

"He's not my stranger," I explain, my voice tinged with exasperation. "He was a customer who came into the bakery looking for a specific pastry but then came back because he thinks I've poisoned him with a love spell!" A gasp escapes her lips, the sharp sound cutting through the noise of the club.

And so, surrounded by the sights, sounds, smells, and feelings of the bustling club, I tell her the whole story of how I met Connor Abernathy.

CHAPTER 8
CONNOR

I wake to my ears ringing and my head throbbing. Rubbing my eyes, I look disorientated around me, trying to piece together what had happened. The rental car's passenger side had slammed against the trunk of a tree, but otherwise, the car seemed intact.

Undoing my seatbelt, I push open the door. As I step out of the car, the air is heavy with the scent of crushed leaves and burnt rubber. The sound of my heartbeat fills my ears, combating the ringing and drowning out the distant chirping of birds. My tongue is coated with the lingering taste of adrenaline, adding to the queasiness in my stomach. The world around me spins, a dizzying blur of colors and shapes. I grip the doorframe tightly, the cool metal grounding me.

The deer who had caught me off guard is nowhere in sight.

First, there was the failed meeting, snapping at Daisy, wrecking the car, and then disconnecting from my brother's call.

Carter!

I slump back into the car seat and feel around for my phone. When I finally grab it, I let out a groan of frustration. The device had flown out of its holder and smashed during the collision. The screen is cracked and flashes in a thousand tiny pixels. Frustration washes over me as I stare at my shattered phone, its broken screen reflecting the shattered fragments of my week.

So much for calling for a ride, let alone my brother back.

With a sinking feeling, I wonder if this string of misfortune is just a cruel twist of fate or something more sinister. At least I don't think I sustained a concussion.

As I limp around the car, my eyes scanning for the extent of the damage, my foot catches on a gnarled root, sending me sprawling onto the rough ground. I land hard, my nose smashing against the unforgiving earth.

"Fuck," I grunt, rolling onto my side and pinching my now bleeding nose.

Could I possibly be so unlucky? What was going on?

As the blood trickling from my nose slows, I glimpse my reflection in the dusty silver rim of the tire. I am a mess. My face is smeared with blood, the dark circles under my eyes are a stark contrast against my pale skin, and my hair is a tangled mess of leaves and debris.

Maybe Daisy is right. Maybe I am working myself to death and could use a vacation.

With a grunt, I push myself off the ground. The passenger side is a mess, but after checking for other issues, the car seems driveable, my ego notwithstanding.

Maybe you're cursed.

"Not funny. The only thing I'm cursed with is your constant input," I say, leaning against the hood of the car as another wave of dizziness and nausea rolls through me.

Definitely a concussion.

It's a good thing you know a pretty nurse. I'm sure she could take care of you. And more than just your bloody nose and bruised ego.

"Shut up," I growl as I wedge myself back into the driver's seat. Each muscle in my body protests as I twist in pain, pulling the seatbelt across my chest. "We're only forty minutes from the airport. We can get cleaned up when we get there."

I turn the key in the ignition and wait.

Nothing.

We could always do it my way and run back on all fours.

"I'm not running to the airport as a wolf and leaving my stuff in the car." I look at the passenger seat floor, where my briefcase has fallen, its contents scattered everywhere: pens, papers, and my broken phone. I yell out in frustration, slamming my fist against the steering wheel. As the car horn blares, a flock of birds, startled from their perch in the trees above, takes flight, their wings a flurry of feathers against the darkening blue sky.

"Come on, car. I need to get to the airport," I say as I turn the ignition.

Nothing. Not even a hum of the motor turning over. Maybe it was more damaged than I could assess from the outside.

I wasn't talking about going to the airport. Where is the fun in that? I was thinking more along the lines of playing nurse and patient.

I pinch the bridge of my nose as I can nearly hear the smile in his voice, wincing at the pain and praying I didn't break it.

"I can't go back. Not only did I leave her—" Wanting and needy. I could smell her arousal, and feel the way she responded to my touch that night. Who knows where it would have led had the phone not rang and given me a second's reprieve to clear my head of her intoxicating taste and smell.

My dick begins to stir at the memory, pressing tight against my slacks.

At least something isn't broken.

She wants us. Go to her.

"I don't know if this is all some elaborate scheme of hers and she's tricked us from day one, wolf." With a groan of frustration, I lean my head back against the headrest, closing my eyes and letting out a weary sigh.

You'll never find out if you don't try. Think of the pack.

"I'm not discussing the pack with you right now." I inhale deeply through my nose.

That's because you don't want to admit I'm right. You don't want to admit that deep down, you were meant to be Alpha. You never even gave your brother a chance to step down.

"Stop." My knuckles blanch as I grip the steering wheel. "That's the past. This is now. What's done is done."

It's not too late for our little nettle.

"She's not *our* anything. For all we know, she's already dating someone." The words taste like ash on my tongue.

You know that's not true. You would have smelt them.

"It doesn't matter. She has her life, and we have ours. The car won't start anyway, and the airport is the shorter route," I say as I pack my stuff back into the suitcase.

Just try. Bat those beautiful blue eyes, click your ruby red slippers, and think of her.

"Third time's the charm, right?" I roll my eyes at his absurdity, but my heart skips a beat as I turn the ignition, and the engine roars to life, a powerful growl erupting from the car's depths. Grinning, I glance up and spot the nearly full moon cresting the treeline in the darkening sky.

I told you so. Now, to our witch?

With a wrench of the steering wheel and a push of the gas pedal, the car jolts forward, the grinding sound of the metal against the tree bark replaced by the squelch of tires finding purchase on the ground.

"We've got business to attend to," I say. I signal my turn toward the airport and press the gas, but the engine coughs and dies, leaving me stranded in the middle of the road. A moment later, a large, gooey splat of bird droppings lands on the windshield with a sickening thud.

"You've got to be fucking kidding me."

I try the ignition, but the car refuses to turn on. Nor have I seen a single car pass this way since I woke up.

Don't mess with fate. This is a sign.

"Fine, you win." I let my thoughts freely think of Netti, the way she fidgets with her apron when she's nervous, the way she nibbles on her bottom lip. Those damnable green eyes of hers.

The engine purrs to life, and I flip a U-turn heading back to Rusthollow.

I PARK outside Magickal Morsels and rush inside.

"Where is she?" I demand the blond-haired woman behind the counter. A couple of patrons seated nearby turn around in their seats to get a look at me, but I don't acknowledge them as I walk over to the register.

"Excuse me? Are you okay? Do I need to call someone for you?" Her eyebrows crease in worry as she looks me over.

"No, I'm fine. There was just a little accident." I wave her off until I catch a glimpse of my reflection. I look like a madman. I couldn't meet Netti looking like this. "On second hand, I need to use your restroom."

Following her direction, I quickly splash water on my face, brushing leaves out of my hair and smoothing it back. It wasn't the best; my clothes are still stained with dirt, but my cuts were already starting to heal, thanks to my shifter magic. When I return to the front of the bakery, she hands me a steaming travel cup of coffee, then leans forward and straightens the top of my button up.

"There you go, much better. Now, who is it you're looking for?" She crosses her arms over her chest.

"Netti. I'm looking for Netti Ellsworth. Is she working today?" I ask impatiently.

Her eyebrow arches in skepticism as she purses her lips, gesturing with a sweeping motion that takes in the entire room. "Does it look like she's here?"

"I *need* her," I say, setting down the coffee and placing my hands on the counter.

"And I need customers to act nicer and a vacation, but I don't see that happening anytime soon." She shrugs and picks at her fingernails.

Connor. My wolf's voice is a low warning rumble in my chest.

"Please tell me where Netti is. It's important I talk to her." I say, attempting to will my body to relax.

"It's her day off," the bakery witch replies.

"What do I have to do to find out where she is?" The desire to see her, inhale her scent, and run my fingers through her hair had become unbearable since I returned. "I need to... apologize for my behavior."

"Well, in that case, she's left town," she replies as she turns around and begins wiping the countertops.

She can't have left.

"Witch," I growl, my hands clenching at my sides. I didn't have time for games like this.

She turns and puts her hands on her hips. "Now, just because you've got some crush on Netti doesn't mean you get to act like some big bad wolf and demand your way into her life. If you really want her, start acting like it."

I stare at her, a bit stunned at her words.

"I'm–I'm sorry. Do you know where Netti is?"

"What did you do that you need to apologize for?" The witch raises an eyebrow.

"I accused her of bewitching me with the scones she made."

Repeatedly on numerous occasions. And then kissed her senseless and left her wanting and needy.

The girl doubles over in laughter, one hand on her chest before meeting my eyes.

"You accused our sweet innocent soon-to-be nurse Netti into cursing you?" She snorts.

"Well, now that you put it that way–"

"I'm sorry wolf-man. I wish I could give you more details because you do seem sincere under that grumpy mask you wear but it's her day off as well as Saturday and Sunday. Normally she picks up the weekend shifts but she says she has a friend in town." She shrugs.

Who is visiting our Nettle?

"I see." My shoulders slump and I sigh in defeat. "Sorry for taking up your time."

The witch leans forward on the counter and taps her fingers on its smooth surface.

"Don't make me regret this. Go get cleaned up. Take the evening to cool down and come back tomorrow afternoon. I start my shift at three. I'll text Netti and see what her plans are tomorrow evening."

CHAPTER 9
NETTI

Picking up the notice of payment due for next semester and looking at my bank statement, my stomach twists. Even with picking up extra shifts at the bakery, it wouldn't be enough to cover what I'd need. After spending the evening talking with Rosemary, who passed out and is sleeping off her fairy gin on the couch, I'd finally convinced myself that maybe it was time to call home and ask for help.

Grabbing my phone, I cringe, imagining how the conversation will go. Mom will tell me she's proud I stuck it out this far, but it's a sign from the universe that it's time to come home. She'll tell me about the nice boys in town who haven't settled down yet and how she could arrange a date through their mothers. Then, she'd launch into a list of my faults and how, if I had just stayed at home, I could have trained at the shop and worked on practicing my magic outside of potions and pastries.

As if I hadn't spent all of my childhood practicing alongside my brothers and cousins.

I can hear the distant sound of cars passing by outside, their tires rolling on the pavement, creating a faint hum. As I prepare for the call, I run a finger along the framed photo of my family, feeling the smooth surface of the glass beneath my touch. The image captures a joyful moment frozen in time. I can almost hear the laughter and excitement that filled the room as we posed for the picture. The memory of our Christmas traditions fills my mind, the sound of my brothers' laughter and the crackling of the fireplace blending together. The smell of freshly baked pastries and the sight of colorful decorations adorning the tree. I can almost taste the sweetness of the treats I used to make.

My brother Ethan took after our great uncle Vernon, who had an affinity for the earth and could coax any plants to grow. Since he was five, he always challenged himself to grow a towering Christmas tree, and we'd all use our magical skills to create decorations. I always baked sweet treats and candies that could be enjoyed on Christmas morning.

But now, as I anticipate my mother's words, the familiar warmth of those memories feels distant, replaced by unease and uncertainty.

I dial the family phone number, my foot tapping a restless rhythm against the floor as the phone rings once, twice. The familiar "Hello?" brings a wave of relief.

"Harrison," I say, a smile spreading across my face as I hear my brother's voice, the one closest to me in age. "Where is Mom and Dad? What are you doing at home today?"

"Well, hello to you too, Netti." The sound of a chair scraping across wooden floors echoes in the background. "Mom and Dad are both at the shop today but they should be home any minute for lunch. Me being home? About that..."

"What did you do this time?" I chuckle. Harrison was always getting himself into situations.

"Well, you know how Mom and Dad like to decorate every year for Christmas? Well, I decided this year I would surprise them by doing the house lights while they were out."

"You and heights are not friends." I shake my head, remembering when he tried to climb up a tree on a dare when he was seven, and I had to climb up and carry him down because he was stuck.

"Poppy Marie was coming by to deliver some tea for mom—"

"And let me guess, you're still crushing on her after a decade and got flustered and tried to show off."

"I was not trying to show off... okay, maybe a little. I was talking to her about how her grandmama was doing while on the ladder. A gust of wind blew in, and I lost my balance and slid down the ladder. I was perfectly fine, except I landed on Mom's English roses and I twisted my ankle trying to gracefully extricate myself."

I let out a loud snort, covering my mouth as my eyes welled up with tears, unable to contain my laughter. "Oh, Harrison, I'd pay good money to have been able to see that. So, you're in a boot for four to six weeks while your ankle heals?"

"Yes, miss 'I'm a smarty pants and decided to leave home to study nursing.' Maybe if you were here, I wouldn't have gotten injured."

"Don't try to put the blame on me," I reply. "You got yourself in plenty of trouble, even when I was home."

"Speaking of, are you coming home for the holidays?" he asks. My cheerful bubble pops. I hadn't been home since I left nearly three years ago.

"You know I can't just up and leave. I have a job and school—"

"Don't you get winter break?" he whines.

"Yes, but the holidays get busy at the bakery," I say. Not only that, but I could use all the extra shifts I could get.

"We miss you," he says.

"I know," I say with a sigh. The sickening feeling of guilt leaves a sour taste in my mouth and a knot in my stomach. "I miss you guys too. I'll be graduating before the summer, though!"

"And then what?"

Then what? That was a good question. I've been so focused on school, work, and bills I hadn't put too much thought into what I'd do afterward. My eyes flick to the flyer on the nightstand before me. Today, there was a job fair at the university for students graduating in the spring. Hospitals, clinics, and packs of magicals looking to hire their own personal nurses and medical assistants would come out. Scholarship and sign-on bonus opportunities are in bold at the bottom of the page.

"Harrison, I'm going to have to let you go. I'll talk to you later," I say as I lift the flyer.

"Didn't you want to talk to the folks?" he says as I hear the muffled voices in the background.

"Yes, but I need to go. I'll call later! Bye, love you!" My resolve is weakening, so I ramble on and end the call before I can change my mind.

"Netti, do you have any ibuprofen?" Rosemary's groggy voice calls from the other room.

"I'll be right there," I reply as I tuck the flier into my pocket.

"I FLY HALFWAY across the country to hang out with you, and you drag me to a job convention?" Rosemary punches me lightly in the arm as she rolls her eyes before opening the rental car door.

"I promise once this is over, I'll take you to my favorite restaurant in the town. I just need to do this." I smile at her before grabbing my bag by my feet and my envelope of resumes. I'd piled my hair back into a neat bun and wore the most demure professional dress I owned, a slack black a-line with matching black heels and the gray scarf Connor had left. It was starting to become chilly, and I didn't want to bring a full cardigan, so I couldn't leave the house without it. There was something about its woodsy scent and luxurious texture that calmed my nerves.

"I know," she says, coming around the car and crushing me into a hug. "I'd do anything to support you. Plus, we have the whole weekend before I have to fly back. This scarf, though, is giving a cozy, chic professional. Is that what you were going for?"

"It's a good luck charm," I reply as I pull back, twisting the ends of the scarf between my fingertips and plastering a smile on my face.

"If you say so." She flicks the tip of my nose and links her arms with mine. "Come on, let's go see what's out there."

We make our way together past the convention hall's doors and into the main area. There appear to be dozens of booths sporting banners of all shapes and sizes, each representing different companies and organizations. The room is buzzing with activity as job seekers and recruiters converse and exchange information. I peer across the room, looking at the names of the booths to get a sense of the opportunities available.

"Welcome to the job fair," a heavy-set middle-aged man to our right says.

Turning, I smile at the stranger and offer my hand. "Netti Ellsworth. Nursing. I graduate in May."

"Fantastic. It's a pleasure to have you here, Miss Ellsworth," he responds warmly. He hands me a pamphlet and gestures around him. "The vendors are distributed around the room, but here is a list of ones specifically looking for nursing." Excited and determined, I take the pamphlet and begin my exploration of the job fair, hoping to find the perfect opportunity to kick-start my nursing career.

"Thank you so much Mr.—" I hesitate.

"Mr. Levatine," he supplies. "Best of luck, Miss Ellsworth."

"Many of these do not look local," Rosemary says as she points to a few booths with well-recognizable logos. "You could find an opportunity to take you anywhere. Maybe even near me."

Her words are lost on me, though, as I see a familiar face across the crowd.

"Netti, what is it?" Rosemary asks, trying to follow my line of vision.

"It's him. The guy I was telling you about."

The jostling crowd surges around me, but I spot Connor instantly, his dark hair, tanned skin, and familiar blue eyes cutting through the chaos. His smile is bright, illuminating his face as he talks to a trio of nursing students standing before him.

"Are you sure?" she whispers, following at my heels as I cut through the room.

"Connor," I say breathlessly as I finally make my way across the room to the table, but his eyes flick from me to Rosemary behind me before lighting up like a kid at Christmas.

"Well, hello there," he says, offering his hand to Rose, but then his eyes flick to me and down to my neck. He reaches out grabbing the trailing edge of my scarf and deeply inhales. His nostrils flare and his pupils dilate.

"Where did you get that?" He drags from my scarf to meet my gaze, his cerulean blue eyes so much like the man I had met, but not quite the same.

Was I losing my mind?

"You're not Connor," I blurt, hand reaching up protectively to the scarf around my throat and stepping back.

"No, I am not." He adjusts the tie around his neck before leaning casually on the table. "Forgive me, your scarf reminded me of someone who used to be part of my pack."

"It's fine." It wasn't fine. My heart races in my chest, fight or flight instincts at this stranger who was so interested in my scarf. Or more pointedly, the man who it belonged to. I clear my throat and smile politely at him. "From a distance, I thought you were someone else." I rub the soft fabric of the scarf between my fingers and thumb.

"That's quite alright. May I ask how you became acquainted with the owner of that scarf?" He raises an eyebrow.

"Oh, it was just a customer who came into the bakery I'm working at while I finish my last semester. Why?" I have the sudden urge to protect a man I hardly knew from the prying questions of this stranger.

"Interesting. I have not seen this pack member in years and was curious what he had been up to. You just caught me by surprise is all. Where are my manners?" He bows at the waist before offering his hand. "I'm Carter, and you two lovely ladies would be?"

I hesitate, reaching out to shake the man's hand, but I don't feel the tingle of recognition as I do when Connor has been in my presence.

"She's Netti, and I'm Rosemary," Rose pipes in. "Can you

tell us about why you're here? My friend Netti here is graduating in May with top honors."

"Well, is that right?" His gaze lingers on her, a mix of curiosity and anticipation evident in his eyes before flicking to me. "I'm Carter Abernathy, the Alpha of the Abernathy clan. Our head healer's assistant recently had to step down due to retirement, and I thought I'd come out to see if anyone would be a good fit for our clan. Understanding, of course, that you'd need an adjustment period for training. We're offering relocation benefits to help with the transition and an upfront stipend upon signing."

He extends a paper toward me, filled with meticulously calculated numbers, causing my throat to tighten. The figures on the paper were more than enough to cover what I owed for my last semester, my rent for the next nine months, and then some. Not only that, but the clan's location was only an hour south of my parents' shop. I'd finally have the opportunity to visit them and my brothers anytime I wanted.

"Mr. Abernathy," I begin, my voice wavering slightly with excitement and uncertainty. I glance between him and the offering in my hand but my mind can't seem to concentrate. Why did he look so similar to Connor? Were they more than just pack mates?

"Please, Netti, call me Carter," he interrupts with a warm smile directed toward both of us. "I don't know what it is about you, but can we talk more about this opportunity over dinner?"

Before I can make a good excuse as to why meeting a stranger for dinner might not be the best idea, Rosemary blurts out, unable to contain her enthusiasm, "That would be lovely! Netti was telling me about this quaint restaurant in town that I've been dying to try while I'm here for the weekend."

A spark of amusement flickers in Carter's eyes as he

glances at me, awaiting my response. "That settles it, then. How does six pm sound?"

CHAPTER 10
CONNOR

After rechecking into the bed and breakfast, I stopped at the store to get a new cell phone. The first thing I try is to call my brother back but his phone goes straight to voicemail.

"Fuck," I say, nearly throwing my new phone at the wall, but I inhale set it down on the table instead.

Good boy. Looks like an old dog can learn new tricks.

"Fuck you," I reply to my wolf half heartedly.

I want to see our Nettle.

"I do too." I glance down at my watch, but it is only 12:30, two and a half hours before the witch is supposed to start her shift.

"Maybe I should buy her flowers? Women like flowers." I pick back up my phone and scroll through maps to see if there is a florist in town.

Maybe you should have spent more time learning about her and less accusing her of cursing you.

I sigh and run a hand through my hair. "You're not wrong."

Wow, are we finally agreeing on something?

"Don't let it go to your head." I grab my keys and wallet off the table.

Kind of hard to do when we share one body.

"I can't stand here waiting until three. There are some shops down near the bakery. I'm sure we can find something for her."

TWO AND A HALF HOURS LATER, I pull up to the bakery right at 3:00 PM. In the back seat is a bouquet of flowers, a box of handmade chocolates, a bottle of wine, a set of journals, and a new set of writing pens.

I rush into the bakery door relieved to see the blonde witch from the day before handing off a parchment bag to

"Any words from Netti?"

Her eyes flick upward, her smile vanishing as she sees me, and a wave of apprehension washes over me as I anticipate the worst.

"She doesn't want to see me," I say to the witch's silence.

"That's not exactly it." She twists her hands before her.

"Then what is it? Where is she?" I tap my foot on the ground, jaw clenched.

"She's—she's on a date."

"A date," I repeat dumbly. I lost her. I had my chance and I blew it.

"Well, it may not be a date. She texted back that she was spending the day at a job fair and that she met someone and thinks things are going to work out and that he asked her out for dinner at 6:00 PM at Noble Noshes," she rambles on.

Dinner at six. That's three hours from now. Maybe we still have time...

No.

"Thank you." I turn on my heel out the door. I sit in the car in the parking lot, shoulders slumped, head hanging. The scent of the bouquet in the backseat is nearly overwhelming, but I can't bring myself to return them or toss them out.

"What do I do?" I say as I pull out and head nowhere in particular. I roll down the windows and let the fresh air in the car as I lose myself to the drive.

She deserves more than the life of a man who is married to his company.

Just as the pack deserved better than us?

"It's not the same," I growl, slamming my fist against the steering wheel.

It's exactly the same. Don't give her up. She needs us as much as we need her. At the very least you need to apologize for your behavior.

I glance at the dashboard where the bright LED light reads 6:15 PM. Have I been so close in my thoughts I've been on autopilot the last few hours?

"What if she doesn't feel the same way?" I say to myself. What if my feelings are just the remnants of a love spell?

I'm going crazy.

You're not crazy. Well, at least not in how you feel about Netti. What are you waiting for?

"True. What have we got to lose?" I turn the car around and punch the address into the car's GPS.

"Estimated travel time, thirty minutes," the electronic voice pipes over the car speakers as I pull onto the main road. The moon, a few days from its peak, ascends in the sky, its face nearly complete, radiating a luminous light on the town around me. My thoughts, however, are completely absorbed by Netti and what I was going to say when I got back to her.

The next thing I knew, I was pulling up to a charming modern restaurant, its silver and black sign proudly proclaiming "Noble Noshes."

I quickly find a parking spot and hurry toward the front door, but I am stopped at the bustling host stand. The hostess, her brow furrowed with concern, shifted her attention from my ragged appearance to the bustling scene behind her, then back to me again.

"Can I help you?"

"Yes, I'm here for dinner." The words spill out of my mouth, and I straighten my cuff sleeves.

"I'm sorry sir, but we are not taking walk-ins at the moment, reservations only."

"I'm meeting someone. They're already here." I stand a little taller, feeling a wave of irritation wash over me. I had never been refused entry to any bar or restaurant, but tonight, I wasn't acting or looking like my usual self.

"I see. Can I have their name?" She pulls out a list.

"Netti Ellsworth," I say, praying she made the reservation.

"Ah yes, here she is. The reservation was nearly an hour ago, though." She frowns, looking at me as though she's seen a ghost.

"There was an accident," I say as I gesture to the nearly healed scratches along my temple. "If you could just point me in the right direction?"

"Of course, right this way, sir." The hostess leads me to a table tucked away in the back of the room, where I immediately spot Netti next to who must be her friend—her pink hair pulled back in a bun and her figure outlined by a clinging black dress. Then, my eyes land on the nearly identical reflection of my face sitting beside her. No wonder the hostess had been confused. She must have thought she was seeing double.

"Carter," I growl, my voice low and intimidating, as I make my way to the table. As I approach, hushed conversations and laughter fade into the background, mingling with the soft music. The clinking of glasses and cutlery adds a discordant note to the already-charged atmosphere.

At the sound of my words, his attention is abruptly torn away from the two women beside him. Their conversation fades into the background, replaced by a deafening silence that hangs in the air as the three of them turn to face me.

What was he doing here, let alone at dinner with my nettle? My skin crawls with a mix of jealousy and anger, a prickling sensation that seems to seep into my very bones.

"Connor?" he asks, his voice cutting through the ambient noise like a sharp blade.

Netti's gaze meets mine and her lips part, eyebrows lifting in surprise. "Connor?"

"Netti, this is your Connor?" Her friend peers over her shoulder at me and whistles. "You didn't tell me he had a twin who looked as good as him." She glances between the two men.

"He's, well he's not—" she stammers.

"What are you doing here?" I ask my brother, my words dripping with disbelief and anger. My fist clenches tightly at my side, my knuckles turning white as I try to contain my mounting rage. The tension in the room is palpable, a heavy-weight that threatens to suffocate us all.

She's ours.

I glance between him and Netti, my eyes darting back and forth like a trapped animal searching for an escape. Netti's breathing quickens, a visible sign of her growing unease. A flush creeps up her cheeks, a rosy hue that hints at her inner turmoil.

My senses are heightened as I feel the pull of my wolf, every detail amplified in this charged moment. The scent of Netti's arousal lingers in the air, a heady mix of desire and temptation and it's all I can do not to act like a jealous barbarian.

"Netti." My eyes settle on her, and I can't help but notice how her dress clings to her, the fabric accentuating every curve of her body. Her nipples, perked and eager, press against the material. "I need to talk to you. Please."

"Connor, you're hurt!" She jumps from her seat and stands on her tiptoes, gently prodding my nose and the scraps along my jaw.

"I'm fine," I say, pulling her wrist close, my lips brushing against its soft skin and inhaling the sweet aroma of vanilla chai tea clinging to her. I'm a tangled web of jealousy, anger, and raw desire—anything but fine. It's left me torn between the urge to grab Netti and whisk her away from Carter and the need to confront him and demand answers.

"You're not fine. What happened?" Her brows draw together in concern.

"There was an accident with the rental car, but I'm fine. I just need to talk to you." My veins feel like molten lava is coursing through them, scorching my insides, while my skin feels like it's about to crack and split. I don't know how long I can control myself without ravishing her.

"How do you know my brother?" Carter's voice chimes in as he stands and puts a hand on Netti's forearm.

He touched our nettle. Brother or not, tear him limb from limb.

"Carter," I growl before inhaling deeply through my nose and exhaling. "Please take your hand off Netti and tell me what you're doing here with her."

He releases his grip, takes a step back, and folds his arms across his chest. I instinctively put an arm around her shoulders, my fingers brushing against her soft hair.

"I'm here in town looking to recruit from the college graduates. Jules is stepping down to retire, and with the growing pack, we need more hands on deck. Something you'd know if you bothered to reach out or come visit us," he accuses. "Netti and I were just discussing the specifics of her contract if she were to accept the job, like a moving fee and sign-on bonus."

I bristle at his words, my heart warring. She needed a job? Money? How much did I not know about this female I could not get out from under my skin? And what would happen if she took a position in a clan I was no longer part of?

"It's nothing set in stone," Netti says, pulling away, and I miss the comforting weight of her against my arm. "You said you needed to talk? It's not about the scones again, is it? I promise—"

I hush her with a gentle finger against her lips, silently shaking my head.

"It's not the scones, and it's not you here having dinner. I was just shocked to see my brother. We haven't exactly seen each other in a few years." He snorts, and I shoot him a glance not to push me.

"You know, Carter. Why don't you and I grab a drink at Taboos and Voodoos? I need to drop the owner a business card," Rosemary says as she loops her arm through Carter's and drags him out the front door, pausing just long enough to turn and wink at us.

I glance around the restaurant before my eyes settle on her.

"I'm sorry," I say, the rest of the words getting stuck in my throat.

"For what?" She nibbles her bottom lip and fidgets with the hem of her skirt.

"Can we talk privately?" I glance again at the people staring at us, at me in my dirty, torn attire.

"Oh, yes, of course. My roommate is gone for the weekend. Rose is staying with me. We can swing by my condo before meeting up with her and Carter–" She glances at the door closing behind them then back at the check where my brother was sitting and winces. "We just need to pay the bill."

Before she can open her purse, I glance at the check, pull three one-hundred dollar bills, and lay them on the table.

"Connor, you didn't have to do that plus that's way more than it cost," she exclaims, eyes widening. "I'm sure Rose and Carter would have paid me back. They just forgot when you showed up and wanted to give us privacy."

"I do, and I did. I behaved terribly the other day and I need to make up for it." I smile, press a hand gently to her back, and lead her to my car.

CHAPTER 11

NETTI

Connor winces as my eyes glance over the damage done to the side of his rental car. Deep scratches mar the paint on the passenger side, and a large dent is impacted into the rear door. My chest tightens as scenarios play through my head. Had he been anything but a shifter, there would be a good chance he wouldn't have walked away from the accident, and we'd be having this conversation as he lay in a hospital bed.

"I'm sorry it's not in the best shape. I got in a little fight with a tree," he shrugs before wrenching open the door and offering me a hand.

As I tuck my feet into the car, I can't help but marvel at the fading bruises and scratches along his jaw. I knew shifters had quick healing abilities, but had never had the opportunity to observe it in real time. This prompts me to question why Carter insisted they needed a healer for their pack and why he was at a job festival nowhere near where the pack lived. It all seems rather coincidental. The door shuts with a click, shattering my thoughts, and Connor slips into the driver's side.

"Netti?" His brows knit together in my silence as he looks at me.

"No, it's not you or this." I shake my head and smile. "It's been a strange week, and I'm just glad the car took the brunt of it."

We drive in silence, the cool winter air seeping through the cracked window, carrying the scent of frost and pine. The gentle hum of the heating system fills the car, competing with the chilly breeze.

"It's just here." I point to the plain brown condo I share with Alita. Connor pulls up front, the tires crunching on the gravel driveway. I rummage in my purse, feeling the smooth leather and the weight of my keys in my hand. We step out of the car, the cold air nipping at our cheeks as we make our way inside. I toss my bag on the beat-up wooden coffee table, the faint scent of old wood lingering in the air. I head into the kitchen, the cool tile floor soothing beneath my feet.

"It's not much—" I begin, but he cuts me off with a husky voice, his words hanging in the air. He leans against the door frame, his hungry eyes fixed on me, their cerulean blue flash golden, like the piercing gaze of a wolf.

"T-ea?" I clear my throat, the sound echoing softly in the small space. I reach for two mugs from the cupboard. The kettle fills at the sink, the sound of rushing water drowning out my racing thoughts. Tea always helps clear my head, and at this moment, with this wolf shifter in my kitchen, it becomes my lifeline, the warm aroma of the steeping tea enveloping the room and blending with the scent of anticipation and desire.

"Netti—" His warm hand wraps around my wrist, and he turns me toward him.

"If this is about the scones," I start but he silences me as he crushes his lips to mine.

"Damn the scones," he growls as his hands fist the fabric of my dress. He leans his forehead against mine and pushes me against the counter. "I can't think when I'm around you, but when I'm not, all I can think of is you. You've bewitched me."

Bewitched him? I hardly have enough control over my magic to do basic spells, let alone conjure up love scones. And to what purpose? I'm too busy for a relationship.

"I have done no such thing. Love spells and lust spells are *illegal,*" I hiss. My body stiffens, and I press my hands against his firm chest to push him away, but it only presses me closer. The evidence of his thoughts presses firmly against my abdomen. Heat pools in my core, and my skin flushes.

His eyes flash open, golden orbs staring into my green, and though I should be afraid of his wolf and the full moon two days away, I feel calm.

"My little nettle," he growls, as one hand tangles in my hair and pulls it back. He nuzzles against the sensitive skin at the column of my neck, his scruff biting at my skin and sending shivers down my spine.

"Connor, I don't even know you."

Even if it were the scones. There is no way their magic is lasting this long. Sure, I'm flattered he was thinking of me, some strange girl when he ate them but the focus charm is NOT this potent. It should last a few hours at most. I should know, I've used them on multiple occasions when studying for a last minute exam. Yet, it's clear this man is fight something.

Goddess only knows I'm fighting my attraction to this man.

Mrs. Taylor's words come hitting me like a brick. 'You have run into your life mate, but something is blocking the bond. Catch him before the next full moon, or else your life will take a turn down a dangerous path.'

There is no way this wolf shifter was my mate. Did witches even have mates?

He continues to stare at me with glossy lust filled eyes.

Maybe just this once, I should give in. What's the harm in one kiss...

I begin to lean on my tip toes when the sound of a sharp whistle pierces through the silence, causing me to jump, my heart pounding. I quickly duck under his arm, my senses heightened, and reach for a pot holder.

"You said you wanted to talk," I manage to say, my voice slightly strained. I clear my throat, the burning sensation from his touch lingering on my skin. The muddled thoughts in my head make it difficult to focus, but we need to address the tension between us. Even though every fiber of my being longs to surrender to him, we must clear the air before things become more entangled.

"Yes," he reluctantly replies, his eyes tracking my every move. His hands hang at his sides, clenched into tight fists, a silent sign of his inner turmoil. I return to the stove, the heat from the burners adding to the charged atmosphere. Carefully pouring hot water into the mugs, I add a tea bag to each one, and the aroma of the brewing tea fills the room. I hand him a cup, the warmth seeping through the porcelain, creating a barrier between us. Holding my cup between both hands, I feel the heat transferring to my palms, providing comfort and grounding. Inhaling the steam rising from the cup, I hope to find clarity amidst the swirling emotions in my mind.

"Tell me what you're thinking." Connor says as he reaches out his free hand and tucks a stray strand of pink hair behind my ear.

Heat infuses my cheeks as I stare over the rim of the cup at him.

That if I wait one minute more before he starts kissing me again, I think I'll go mad. No, that's too rash.

"I'm always thinking." I pause, taking a sip and he stares at me incredulously.

"Clearly."

"What's that supposed to mean?" My eyebrows raise in mock offense.

"That in the short time I've known you–you're always working. You seem like someone that is always on the go, always sacrificing for others."

"You don't know me." I step back.

"I know people, Netti. I wouldn't get where I have without knowing people." He steps forward, his hand gently cups my cheek. "And for some reason, I feel like I *really know* you. To a point where it drives me mad."

"You haven't known me long enough to determine how I feel."

"You look exhausted, Netti." His thumb caressing the skin beneath my eyes, a tender gesture that undoubtedly reveals the sleepless nights I've endured over the past few days, leaving their mark on my face.

"That's not very nice," I say, my voice coming out barely a whisper.

"Who says I'm a nice guy?" he growls, his voice dripping with menace. The words hang in the air, each syllable pronounced with an ominous tone. Slowly, he leans closer, his breath tickling my earlobe. A shiver runs down my spine as his lips graze the delicate shell of my ear.

I can't help but feel a wave of warmth coursing through me, my body almost melting into his presence. But as quickly as the moment comes, he pulls back, his eyes still burning with intensity. He sets his cup down in the sink with a clank, the sound reverberating in the silence that follows.

"There is something we need to discuss," he says, his voice tinged with urgency. The words hang heavy in the air, a palpable tension filling the room. "I need you to take this spell off me."

"What?" I step back, unable to contain the laughter that bubbles up within me. It escapes my lips, filling the space around us with a lightness that contrasts the gravity of his words.

He looks at me, his expression serious, unyielding. "This is not a joke," he insists, his voice breaking through my laughter. I can see the desperation in his eyes, a flicker of uncertainty amidst the intensity. His words hang in the air, a heavy cloud of concern.

"I feel cursed," he continues, his voice wavering. The weight of his words settles upon me, sinking into my bones. I can almost taste the bitterness of his frustration, the tang of helplessness. Regret at my laughter curdles in my gut. "Not to mention, I hardly have control over my wolf." At that moment, as if spurned on by the rising emotions, Connor's eyes flash golden.

Crossing my arms over my chest, I frown, the gesture accentuating the tension in the room. The scent of determination fills the air, mixing with the faint aroma of uncertainty. I can feel the weight of his accusation pressing against my conscience.

"I don't deal in curses or love spells," I say firmly, my voice laced with conviction. The words hang in the air, a shield against his doubts.

"So you've said before." He taps his foot impatiently on the floor.

"What else do you want me to say?" My lips press into a firm line.

"There is something bigger going on here than just your

damned pastries." Connor's eyes narrow, his gaze piercing as he takes a step closer. "Just tell me, how do you know my brother?" His voice is sharp, cutting through the tension. The words hang in the air, a demand for answers.

I throw my arms wide, a gesture of exasperation. "He was here for a job fair," I explain, my voice tinged with frustration. "Anything else you need to know, Mr. Bossy Grumpy Pants?" The words escape my lips before I can stop them. I cover my mouth with my hands, my eyes widening in realization. The taste of mortification lingers on my tongue, an unwelcome flavor in the air.

I did not just let that slip.

Connor stares at me as though I've grown a third head. His gaze filled with disbelief. I watch as he absorbs my words, his eyes locked on mine. The silence stretches, a heavy cloak enveloping us both, punctuated only by our breathing. The atmosphere is thick with awkwardness, suffocating yet undeniably palpable.

Yep, I definitely let that slip out.

Connor tosses back his head and starts laughing.

That's it, I've broken him.

"Connor?" I lay a hand on his forearm, my half-finished cup of tea forgotten on the counter. "I'm sorry. I don't know what came over me?"

"Sorry?" He shakes his head before putting either hand on the side of my face and pressing his lips against mine until we both pull away, gasping and breathless. "No one has dared talk to me like that since my brother and I were pups."

"I didn't mean to—" I begin, but he silences me with another kiss, fingers weaving through my hair. I arch into his touch, my embarrassment melting away like chocolate replaced with need.

"No more talk of curses or spells. Magical influence or not. I want nothing but to spend the evening learning more about you." His free hand drifts down my back, pulling me close and molding our bodies together. "That is, if you don't have any other plans tonight?"

"Rosemary."

"If I know my brother, she won't be coming back here until tomorrow. We can meet them for a second breakfast."

"Second?"

"Yes." He lifts me, and I wrap my legs around his waist. He carries me toward my bedroom. "Because I'll be having my first serving before we even leave to meet them in the morning."

He sets me down at the edge of the bed and kneels between my feet. His hands stray from my waist, leisurely down the length of my calf until he stops at my ankles, taking his sweet time undoing the laces.

"Now tell me what you want, my nettle." He presses a kiss to the inside of my bare knee as he slips one boot off and then the other. A soft moan escapes my lips as his fingers work their magic, relieving the tension in my feet. I close my eyes, letting my head fall back in pure bliss. "Tell me what you want, and I shall give it to you."

What do I want? A tricky question with too many answers, but at the moment, all of them seem trivial except one. I want him. All of him. This man I just met but feel as though I've known for eons.

Warmth blossoms in my core and spreads through my veins at the thought. I open hooded eyes as Connor pauses, nostrils flaring as though he can smell my desire.

"What are you thinking?"

"That we're doing too much talking and not enough doing."

He's right though. There is something going on here. Something more than just magic.

Feeling brazen and bold, like I've never felt in the bedroom, I gently push him so he sits on the floor. I slide off the bed and kneel before him. With shaky fingers, I undo the buttons of his shirt. I untuck it from his pants, then slide it off his broad shoulders, letting my fingers trace the contours of muscles on his chest under a dusting of dark hair.

His breath deepens as he watches me, hands braced beside him on the floor. He holds still, muscles tense as if giving me time to explore and waiting for permission to touch me more. My fingers skim the edge of his pants, and the length of him strains against the soft gray fabric.

"I want you to take it off. I want to see you," I whisper, my voice heavy with desire. The words leave my mouth as I tug at his leather belt, the anticipation building between us.

"As you wish," he replies, his voice husky with longing. He cups my face and kisses me gently, his lips igniting a fire within me before pulling me with him to stand.

Standing, his presence towers over me, commanding attention and sending a shiver of excitement down my spine. As he loosens the confines of his pants and kicks them to the side, his dick springs up, proudly on display. I gaze down from his hungry eyes to his muscular legs, unable to tear my eyes away from this perfect specimen of masculinity. How can a man be built this way?

My heart catches in my throat as I take in every inch of the man standing before me. His chiseled features, the slight stubble on his jawline, the confidence radiating from his piercing eyes—it all overwhelms me, making me weak in the knees. I can't help but reach out, my fingers trembling as I drag them down the ridges of his torso to trace the curves and valleys of his sculpted physique. He takes a deep, shuddering breath, mirroring the intensity of my desire, and I realize we are both consumed by an insatiable hunger for one another.

I've seen men naked before. I've even had a few withering relationships, but I never gave myself permission to look openly, then. I do now.

His length is hard under my gaze. His arousal is obvious.

My insides clench as I drag a finger down the length of him, marveling at how it twitches under my examination. I wrap my hand around him, eliciting a gasp. He's much larger than anyone I've been with. Much larger than I expected. My heart beats faster in my chest as an ache grows between my legs.

"Netti," he growls against the shell of my ear. "Tell me what you want. A man can only have so much patience."

I giggle at the thought of making him lose his patience. He pulls back, and I prepare for a grumpy remark, but his eyes dance with mischief. His kiss is deep and lingering, his mouth moving against mine with a slow, lazy passion while his hand tangles possessively in my hair.

"I want…" I murmur against his lips.

"Tell me," he whispers, his hand drawing circles on my lower back.

"You know it's not fair…" I trail off as he nips at my neck. The feeling of his teeth against my skin sends a jolt of pleasure through me, making me gasp and arch into his touch. "That I'm naked, and you're still fully clothed?"

A wicked grin spreads across his face, and with a deafening rip, his claws tear through the back of my dress and bra. The shredded fabric of the dress pools around my feet, revealing my light pink lacy underwear.

"That was my favorite dress," I gasp. My nipples pebble as I stand before him.

"I'll buy you a hundred more." He steps forward, his

warmth surrounding me. The back of my thighs hit my bed. "Now, tell me what you want."

"I want..." I take a shaky breath, unused to voicing my desires.

Magic or not. I want this man. I want him more than I've wanted anyone ever. Even if just for tonight. He might see it as a curse, but I can't deny the chemistry we share; it's ignited an insatiable need inside me.

"I want you to touch me. I want to feel good and not have to worry."

"Nettle, you're perfect. You never have to worry with me." He kneels, hands braced on my hips, and meets my gaze. "You have to promise me that if I do something you don't like, if you want to stop, you will tell me."

"Yes." Somehow deep inside, I know he will not do anything to harm me, and neither will his wolf.

"Good." He leans forward and flicks his tongue against my nipple, eliciting a moan. His hand trails down my waist between my legs before stroking my clit. I writhe under his touch as he slips a finger into me, curling until he hits a sweet spot that sends waves of pleasure coursing through me.

"Connor," I plead, writhing under him as he slips another finger in, slowly building up a tempo.

"Come for me," he demands, repositioning himself and picking up his pace. The scruff of his jaw against my inner thigh sends sensations I've never felt before coursing through me. My body arches as I feel the heat of his breath at my core. I reach the peak, crying out. "Good girl," Connor whispers against my skin staring up at me.

He kisses my inner thigh, pulling out and wrapping his hand around his dick, pumping it once, twice. His body leans in, his erection grazing against me as he playfully nibbles on my left breast.

"Wait," I gasp as he gives attention to my other breast, kneading it in his palm and pinching the nipple between his fingers. "In my nightstand. Condoms."

He reaches over and opens the drawer before chuckling. "Those won't fit me, love." He turns and rummages through his discarded pants until he retrieves a gold foil-wrapped square. He makes quick work, rolling the condom up his length before returning to my side.

Kissing me softly, he guides himself to my entrance.

He holds my gaze as he slowly pushes. As he fills me, a soft groan escapes his lips. A brief, sharp pang of pain makes me tense, my breath catching in my throat. He feels impossibly big, and I worry he will not fit.

Connor stills, resting his weight on his forearms on either side of my head. He's breathing hard, his biceps clenched and his expression strained. He nuzzles at the side of my face and my body starts to adjust to him. His movements are deliberate, each one a slow, deliberate dance, and the pinch of pain blossoms into a strange pleasurable sensation. Something I want more of. Pressure and friction and the feeling of being completely filled by him.

I grip his shoulders, sinking my fingers into the muscle as he increases his rhythm. Every nerve in my body seems to vibrate, my heart hammering against my ribs as I'm consumed by a torrent of new sensations and feelings.

As if sensing the change in me, he pushes until he's fully seated inside. His hand slides into my hair as his mouth claims mine, and he rolls his hips. Moaning, I open myself fully for him, my nails raking along his back.

"I've been dreaming about doing this since the day I met you." He dips to my throat, where he kisses, sucks, and nibbles. His voice is strained as he whispers into my ear. "I've wanted you. Thought of nothing but you."

"Show me." I sink my teeth into his bottom lip as he kisses me, tempting to provoke his wolven side.

He growls and plunges into me hard. I cry out, arching against him. Pain and pleasure mingle together.

"Fuck." He clenches his fist beside my head and moves to pull out, but I hook my legs around him.

"More," I beg, tilting my hips to take him deeper. I'm so close to reaching my peak.

His eyes gleam feverishly golden, and it's as if I'm looking directly at the wolf. He groans, shoulders relaxing under my fingertips.

"Demanding little creature." He nips at the shell of my ear.

"You told me you'd give me what I want."

"So I did," he said, thrusting into me with force and depth. In response, I tighten my legs around his waist and curl my ankles around his back. The change in pressure and friction enhance the sensations within me, reaching new heights I never knew existed.

"You're so fucking beautiful," he murmurs, his words resonating deep within me. The delicious tension builds as he moves deeper and faster, and I find myself craving more. Writhing beneath him, I can't get enough. "Look at me, my nettle," he commands, and I obediently bring my eyes back to his.

With one final plunge, he pushes me over the edge, and a surge of release washes over me, causing me to cry out. I unravel completely beneath him, and moments later, he groans as his muscles spasm above me, thrusting one last time.

"Fuck, Netti," he exclaims, finally stilling before pulling out and collapsing next to me. He nestles his face into the nook between my neck and shoulders, inhaling deeply. My hand rests on his chest, feeling his heart pounding. Although there are more things I want to discuss with him, the weight of sleep overcomes me, and I drift off into slumber.

CHAPTER 12
CONNOR

My body jolts awake, and I crack open my eyes, staring at the unfamiliar room until my gaze settles on the light magenta-haired woman snuggled up on my chest.

Mine.

The words resonate in my chest, and I'm not sure if they come from my wolf or my own consciousness. I carefully extricate myself from under her arm, watching as she curls up under the blanket. Her lashes cast shadows across her cheekbones from the morning light peeking in through the window. I glance at my watch on the nightstand, shocked to find it is nearly 9:30 in the morning. My stomach rumbles with hunger, reminding me I'd slept through breakfast. My fingers run through my tangled hair as I scan the room, searching for my clothes, scattered and abandoned last night. I can't remember the last time I slept in past 6:00.

As I pull on my pants, I chance another glance at Netti, who is curled up asleep on the bed. For that matter, when was the last time she slept this good? Her expression is soft in sleep, with no worry creasing her brow, and gone were the dark circles under her eyes.

Feed her. She deserves it after last night.

I roll my eyes at my wolf as I button up my shirt and tuck it into my waistband before tightening my belt. But his words nag at me, followed by the desire to protect her. She was just a woman. One that last night was supposed to get out of my system and move on from. But the more I thought about last night, the more I knew I was in trouble. Last night was just a taste of Netti. Now I am addicted, and she is my drug. I glance back at her sleeping form before heading to her dresser to grab my phone and wallet. I'll slip out and grab her some coffee and breakfast before she wakes up.

That's when my eyes snag on the bills spread out across the wooden surface. My chest constricts as I pick up the letters one by one. The first is stamped with a tuition payment due date followed by the information that if payment was not received she'd be dropped from her program. It becomes clear to me that Netti is struggling to make ends meet. Flipping through the rest of the envelopes, guilt tangling in the pit of my stomach at going through her mail but unable to stop myself, I discover overdue bills with late fees, bills for books and supplies. The weight of her financial burden hits me hard, and I realize she has been quietly dealing with this on her own.

I drop the envelopes and they hit her mouse, lighting up her computer. Bright on the screen reads the line "Connor Abernathy, CEO of Abernathy Inc., scores a multimillion-dollar project that skyrockets business to a new level." My stomach drops, and I step away, feeling my world shatter. Netti had said she had no motivation to trick me into falling for her. She had said she didn't even know who I was, but what better proof against that than the bills scattered across her desk and multiple tabs about me on her computer?

The realization hits me like a ton of bricks. Netti must have known who I was and deliberately kept it hidden. The depth of her deception cuts deep, and I'm torn between anger and a strange sense of admiration for her resilience. She didn't want me to know about her financial struggles, and she certainly didn't want me to help her out of pity.

Connor, you're thinking too far into this.

Ignoring him, I slam the door behind me as I storm out the front door, letting my fury reverberate through the house. I'm feeling overwhelmed and need to find some solitude to clear my head.

You're acting like an animal, and I'm the canine here.

"Shut the fuck up for once," I growl, getting into the rental car and slamming into reverse.

If she was so interested in your money, why is she killing herself working overtime? Clearly, the evidence is written all over her face at how hard she's trying to make ends meet. Plus, why was she at the job fair?

"Carter." Jealousy flairs hot inside me, and the edge of my vision dances red as I turn onto the main street, trying to put as much distance between myself and Netti as possible. I still haven't figured out why my brother was here—in this small town, of all places, looking for a nurse—but I was going to find out. I punch in his number, the phone ringing over the car's speakerphone.

"Hello?" Carter's voice is sleepy as he answers the call.

"Where are you?" I make a sharp right turn, the engine roaring as I accelerate down the winding road.

"I'm at my hotel." He yawns, and I hear a female mumble in the background. "Why? Where are you?"

"What hotel?" My hands grip the steering wheel until my knuckles blanch. I don't have time to play these games.

"At the Lakefront hotel five minutes south of EnchanTea on the lake's edge, why?"

"I'm on my way—"

A loud *pop bang* echoes through the air before the car sputters to a halt, thick white steam billowing from the engine.

"Fuck!" I roar, slamming my fist against the steering wheel, the horn blaring in a jarring, angry blast.

You need to go back to her.

"No, I don't."

"What did you say? What's going on, Connor?" My brother's voice calls broken over the car's speaker.

"Nothing. Sorry. My wolf... he's acting up," I reluctantly admit.

"Ok, but that doesn't explain the deafening bang I just heard. Are you branching off into bombs now?" He exclaims with a half-hearted joke.

I switch the phone to speaker mode, the call echoing in the car as I step out onto the pavement. The acrid smell of burnt rubber and the hiss of steam assaults my senses, causing me to wrinkle my nose in disgust. The unmistakable scent of trouble fills the air, mingling with the faint smell of gasoline. "No. But I wish I had paid more attention when Uncle Ron was showing us car repair instead of focusing on business," I mutter, frustration tainting my voice.

"Do you need my help?" His offer hangs in the air, a lifeline I couldn't bring myself to grasp.

Help.

The word echoes in my mind, a reminder of my resistance to relying on others. I step back, distancing myself not just physically but emotionally, from the pack, from him, from my family. Years of separation have left me isolated, a lone figure in a vast and unforgiving world. I was numb to it until I stepped into this small town.

Even though anger still courses through my veins at Netti's possible betrayal, I can't ignore the empty ache that fills the void she has left behind. The memory of her intoxicating scent and tender touch lingers, haunting me in my solitude.

Should I have stayed, instead of storming out like an insolent pup?

Do you want me to answer that?

"Connor?" my brother asks.

"Sorry, it looks like something blew or burned in the engine."

"Where are you? I'm coming to get you," he says.

"You don't need to. I'll call a tow truck and a cab."

I let out a heavy sigh and lean against the car, only to yelp as my hand makes contact with the scorching metal. I recoil, my hand instinctively pulling away, and stare at the bright pink flesh, the stinging pain making my brows furrow.

You need to go back to the girl. Clearly, we're cursed without her.

"Cursed with her, without her. What is it, wolf?" I growl, a low rumble in my chest. I look around the deserted street, lined with tall green pines and vibrant burgundy maples.

"Connor." My brother's tone is commanding and low, reminiscent of our father. "We need to talk."

His words hang heavy in the air. About the pack? The girl?

"Fine." I punch in the GPS location, send it to him, and then end the call before dialing a tow truck. Let him fume over being hung up on. I had questions and this conversation was a long time coming.

Ten minutes later, my brother pulls up, followed by the tow truck. He loops his thumbs through his belt loops, letting out a low whistle as he stares at my rental car being loaded onto the truck.

"Who did you piss off? You're lucky if it needs anything less than a total." He smirks and gestures to his car. "Come on. Let's go get some coffee."

Where is Netti's friend? She'll skin us alive if he's hurt her.

"Where is Netti's friend?"

"Oh, Rose?" The corner of his lips turn up before he punches me in the shoulder. "She's sleeping in, as I should be instead of rescuing your ass. Don't worry, she's safe and in one piece. I'm sure the girls are already making plans for lunch."

We ride in silence to EnchanTea and then order two black coffees, the rich, bold aroma enveloping us as we receive our steaming cups. We find a secluded table in the back, away from the bustling chatter of other patrons.

"Why are you in Rusthollow?" we both say in unison, our voices barely audible above the soft background music. Carter chuckles and shakes his head before taking a deep swig of his coffee, the sound of the liquid being swallowed echoing in the quiet space.

"I miss seeing your face. Mom misses you," he says. He gives me a pointed look.

"You know why I can't come back. You know we wouldn't last one week before we're at each other's throats," I reply, my voice tinged with resignation. I stare at the swirling black liquid in my cup, the steam rising and dissipating into the air, carrying a sense of uncertainty with it.

"It doesn't have to be that way," Carter starts, his voice filled with hope.

"It's the laws of nature. We were always born to bear the burden, one to rise to Alpha, the other to leave," I snap, my frustration seeping into my words. Suddenly, my coffee spills over the edge of my cup, the warm liquid splashing onto the table, creating a small puddle.

"Shit. I'm sorry," I mutter, regret lacing my words.

"Connor, you left us," he accuses, his voice filled with pain and anger.

"I was not going to fight you, hurt you," I defend myself, feeling my wolf stir under my skin. I meet his gaze, his face a mirror image of mine, the resemblance uncanny.

"You never asked if I wanted to be Alpha. You didn't even give me a chance to step down," he accuses.

"You don't want to be Alpha?" I ask. A thousand questions filling my mind. How did I not see that all the years growing up. We had always done everything together, sports, hobbies. I presumed he wanted the role as Alpha just as much as I did.

Perhaps you projected your wants on him, instead of letting him find his own path.

"No," Carter says, taking a sip of his coffee. He absentmindedly strums his fingers on the table. "I never wanted to lead the pack. I knew I didn't have what it took," he admits, the weight of his confession hanging in the air.

"You're doing a fine job—" I begin, my words interrupted by his snort, the sound cutting through the quiet ambiance. He slams his fist on the table, the sudden impact causing a jolt in the atmosphere.

"That's because of *your* support. Don't you think I know where the anonymous donations come from?" he says. He quirks an eyebrow at me before continuing, his words laced with sarcasm. "You could have used a less obvious name than Abernathy Inc."

"I—You have a point. But you are doing a great job as Alpha. The pack is thriving, the people are happy."

"What's going on with you and the girl?" he says, changing the subject.

Netti.

My stomach drops, jealousy clouding my thoughts. "Calm down, Connor," Carter says reassuringly, laying a hand on my forearms where claws have lengthened from my hands. "I have no intention of courting her. I have my eyes set on another." He glances at the phone sitting on the table, his expression pensive.

Curiosity piqued, I inquire, "Why are you here in Rusthollow, then? There must be dozens of other schools and job fairs closer to home."

"To be honest," Carter sighs, leaning back in his chair and placing his hands behind his head, "the flyer showed up at the pack headquarters the day Jules put in her retirement. I tossed it in the trash with the rest of the junk mail, but I couldn't stop thinking about it. So, the next morning, I pulled it out and reached out to the fair to secure a spot. I had no idea you'd be here. Why are you here, anyway?"

"I came to town to secure a deal for a big building project, but I've messed it up," I confess, weariness evident in my voice. I rub my face wearily before sharing the details of my week's disasters, like we used to do when we were pups.

"So now, anytime you're away from her, disaster seems to strike?" Carter observes, setting his empty mug on the table.

I nod, feeling a mix of frustration and helplessness.

"But you're afraid she's known all along, and someone put her up to this ruse?"

"Now that you put it that way, it sounds ridiculous," I admit.

At least someone is thinking logically. My wolf snorts in agreement inside my head.

"Well, you know what you need to do now?" Carter says.

"What?"

"Win the girl, fix the deal, and come take your rightful

place as Alpha," he declares, a wolfish grin spreading across his face.

CHAPTER 13
NETTI

Warm morning light dances across my face, casting a soft glow on the room. As I slowly awaken, the memories of last night start to come into focus. I shift in bed, my hand instinctively reaching out for Connor, but all I feel is the cold, wrinkled fabric of the sheets. Confusion creeps into my mind, and my brows furrow as I realize he is not here.

"Connor?" I call out but only silence reaches my ears.

I sit up, scanning the room for any sign of his presence, but the only evidence of his visit is the torn condom wrapper on my nightstand table. A mix of disappointment and frustration washes over me as I realize that perhaps I had expected more from him, only to be left with an empty bed and a lingering regret. His scent still lingers in the air, a constant reminder of the passionate moments we shared. I find myself cursing at my naivety, acknowledging that he was likely just looking to satisfy his desires and move on.

"Fucking shifters," I mutter under my breath, a hint of bitterness seeping into my voice.

With a sigh, I fall back onto the pillow, exhausted.

As I lay there, another thought crosses my mind, causing a pang of concern. Rose, my best friend, had also been with me last night, but I hadn't seen her since she left with Carter. A sudden worry grips my heart, and I reach for my phone on the nightstand. With a sinking feeling in my stomach, I unlock the screen, only to find it devoid of any notifications. The absence of messages or calls from Rose intensifies my unease, fueling my growing dread. Something isn't right, and I can't shake the feeling that there's more to last night's events than meets the eye.

> Hey, just checking in. Everything alright?

A few moments later, my phone buzzes with her reply.

> OMG, once you go wolf, you can't go back. We're going to grab coffee. How was your night?

> So you and Carter are a thing?

> We will see. You know I don't do long distance relationships. How was your night?

A wave of anger washes over me, leaving my cheeks burning as I start typing a response, then quickly delete it, unable to find the right words. How do I describe I had the best night of my life only to wake up alone?

A wave of fear crashes over me, leaving me breathless and trembling, and instantly it's followed by a surge of rage, hot and powerful. My heart pounds in my ears, my breath catches in my throat, and the phone, suddenly heavy in my hand, plummets to the floor, the impact echoing in the silence. The acrid smell of smoke and burnt rubber fills my nostrils. A strange buzzing fills my ears. A disorienting hum that quickly subsides, leaving behind a strange, almost unsettling silence.

What was that?

I rub at the center of my chest where the strange feelings had originated. It was as if, for a moment, I was somewhere else, feeling someone else's feelings.

But how could that be?

My phone buzzes again, vibrating on the floor and I scoop to pick it up.

Netti? Is everything alright?

Yeah, I'm fine. Just tired. See you for lunch?

Sounds good, where at?

I type out the address of my favorite Thai restaurant in town, before hitting send. The aroma of spicy and aromatic Thai cuisine wafts through my imagination, making my mouth water in anticipation. When was the last time I treated myself?

Feeling determined and empowered, I refuse to wallow in self-pity if Connor decided he wanted a one-night stand and was out. I pace in a circle, trying to untangle my thoughts and dismiss my disappointment. As the warm sunlight filters through the window, casting a gentle glow on my bedroom, I stand before the mirror and admire my reflection as I run my fingers through my hair, half cascading down in loose curls and the other half elegantly pulled up.

With a graceful swipe, I apply a coat of mascara to my lashes, enhancing their natural beauty. I apply a small amount of my favorite burgundy lip gloss, a subtle hint of berries, and gently press my lips together. A surge of confidence fills me as I select my outfit, the soft fabric of my pink dress brushing against my fingertips as I slide it off the hanger. The dress, with its demi-puffed sleeves and a low neckline, hugs my curves and flares out in a twirlable skirt that reaches just above my knees.

"Come on, Honey." I whistle as I grab my phone and purse. My fruit bat companion, perched on his branch nearby, senses my excitement. He spreads his wings and gracefully glides toward me, landing gently on my head. I can feel the delicate weight of his body as he curls around my bun, his presence adding a touch of whimsy to my ensemble.

Perfect.

FIFTEEN MINUTES LATER, I reach the edge of Basil Brilliance, a quaint little restaurant known for its exquisite cuisine. As I approach the door, I immediately spot Rosemary's rental parked nearby. The door to the restaurant chimes and an elderly gentleman greets me with a bow.

"Welcome to Basil Brilliance. Will you be dining alone?" he asks politely.

I shake my head and reply, "No, I'm meeting a friend—" Just as I say that, my eyes land on Rose, sitting next to Carter and waving excitedly at me from their table in the dining hall. A warm smile spreads across my face as I spot her. I thank the gentleman and make my way toward their table.

Rose jumps up, her enthusiasm evident as she wraps me in a tight bear hug that almost takes my breath away. After releasing me, she holds me at arm's length and admires my appearance.

"Netti, this is just lunch. You didn't have to go all out.

Unless, of course, a certain wolf shifter is joining us," she teases, winking mischievously. My stomach sinks at her words, and my gaze shifts nervously between Rose and Carter.

How do I tell her what happened between me and Carter's brother? How will he react if he finds out? I decide now is not the time to jeopardize our meeting by revealing the truth.

I smile and turn to face Carter, mustering the courage to bring up the job opportunity we had discussed.

"He's not, but I would like to discuss that job opportunity." Carter's eyes light up like a child on Christmas morning, and he flashes me a wide grin. At that moment, I momentarily forget that I'm looking at him and not his brother as memories of our passionate encounter from last night flood my mind.

"Netti?" Rose's voice cuts through my thoughts. She clears her throat and gestures to the waiter. We are seated at a cozy corner table in a bustling Thai restaurant, surrounded by the tantalizing aroma of spices and the hum of conversation.

"Sorry." I shake my head and smile at the two of them. "It's been a long week." The waiter approaches, and Rosemary and Carter place their orders. As he turns to me, I grab the menu and scan through the list of options.

"Just a chicken Thai basil with brown rice, please. Oh, and a Thai tea with boba." The waiter jots down my order and heads back to the kitchen. Boba Thai tea is one of my favorite treats and something I rarely indulged in, but after this whirlwind week, I need comfort food.

"How was the club?" I ask, fiddling with the edge of my skirt.

My friend, with a mischievous grin, responds, "Oh, it was fabulous. I was just telling Carter about how I knew he'd be impressed with Taboos and Voodoos. I even suggested he fly out and spend an evening at Luminous Lounge, the popular spot in my neighborhood." She winks at him teasingly. "But then again, Netti, you should come too," she continues. "Your whole life is about to change in a few months. Can you believe you're only a semester away from graduating? I'm so proud of you." Her words warm my heart. She reaches over and squeezes my hand.

"That sounds like fun, Rose." As much as I appreciate her praise, a slight unease settles within me. I know I possess the knowledge, skills, and determination to finish my degree, but there is one major obstacle standing in my way: the burden of my loans and bills. Graduating seems like an impossible dream unless I can find a way to pay them off.

The waiter arrives with our food, steaming bowls of curry and fragrant rice. I take a long sip of my tea, relishing in the sweet, creamy flavor.

"So, you're interested in the job?" Carter asks, lacing his fingers and staring at me over the table. My heart pounds in my chest, and my palms grow damp. I discreetly wipe them on my skirt, trying to appear calm and collected.

"Yes, I've given it much consideration and think I'd be a good fit." I try to sound confident, but deep down, doubt creeps in. What would I say qualifies me above the other candidates? I haven't even considered that there could be others vying for the position, especially given the salary that was posted.

"Unfortunately, she won't be able to take your job offer, as better opportunities have arisen elsewhere," Connor says, slipping beside me and slipping an arm around my shoulders. My heart skips a beat, and I turn to face him, surprise evident in my eyes. "That is, if she will accept my proposal to come on to Abernathy Inc. I've been looking for someone to lead our new HR and health section."

The words hang in the air, and my mind races to process the unexpected turn of events. Abernathy Inc. is Connor's renowned company with a reputation for excellence. The opportunity to lead a new department and make a significant impact on employee well-being. It's a tempting proposition, and I can feel my excitement building.

Then, I remember the events of the morning.

"Wait, what?" My brows draw together in confusion. My heart is a battleground of confusion, yearning, and anger.

"I'm sorry I left so abruptly this morning. I needed to... sort some things out," he admits, but his free hand makes its way to my knee, circling the sensitive flesh in slow, tantalizing movements.

"Is that so?" Carter drawls, his fingers tapping a staccato rhythm on the table, his impatience evident.

"Yes, it is," Connor replies, and the tension in the air is nearly palpable. "What makes you so sure Netti even wants to accept your proposal?" He smiles wolfishly across the table at his brother. "What if she would prefer to be part of the pack?"

Connor, beside me, stiffens, his fingers tightening possessively on my thigh, sending a jolt of awareness through me. Heat pools between my legs as my body betrays me, weakening my resolve against the man who left so abruptly this morning.

"How do you know she wants to be part of the pack? She hardly knows you," Connor challenges.

"And she knows you better?" Carter laughs, leaning back in his chair with his arms behind his head. "I hardly say knowing her a few days longer makes you any less of a stranger."

"What did you offer her to make her uproot her entire life to accept?" A muscle twitches in Connor's jaw.

"I came to talk to Carter about the job proposition. He didn't force me or bribe me." I turn in my seat, but as I meet Connor's gaze, a sense of possibility fills the space between us. Deep within my chest, I feel a connection and feelings I can't explain. The long week suddenly feels like a distant memory, replaced by the potential for a new chapter in my career. But would that be enough? What if I give up everything I worked the last few years for just to be disappointed? I need to think. I need fresh air.

"Netti isn't a plaything to be squabbled over," Rosemary declares, her lips pressed together in a tight line as she rises from the table. "Let's let these two get whatever this is out of their system."

CHAPTER 14

CONNOR

*M*ine.

The word rumbles somewhere deep and primal inside me.

Don't let our mate get away.

Mate. The impossible word resonates in my head, and I realize I've been a bigger fool than I thought. How did I not see all the signs?

"Netti, wait." I run to her side and grab her hand as they reach Rosemary's car. She stops, turning around to face me, her emotions playing like an open book over her face. "I'm sorry."

"You left." The words are a punch to my gut as she pulls out of my grasp and stares up at me.

"I—" My throat tightens, and suddenly I feel at a loss for words. How could I express my feelings when I can't even admit it to myself? I want her. I want the pack.

Pull yourself together. Tell her.

"I knew it wasn't going to work, Connor." She pastes a smile on her face that doesn't meet her eyes.

"Netti, that's not it."

"Our lives are too different, Connor. You have your path, and I need to make mine."

"Netti," I plead, my chest constricting painfully.

Tell her the truth.

"I panicked, okay? When I got up, I saw all the bills on your dresser and your computer open to tabs about me and my business. I thought you had lied to me about your involvement in the spelled scones. I thought maybe because of your financial situation, you were given an opportunity by a rival trying to ruin this deal for me," I explain, my voice filled with regret.

She steps back, hurt and anger evident on her face. Behind us, I hear my brother approaching and notice Rosemary standing rigidly near the driver's side of the car.

"You went through my things?" she asks, her voice filled with disbelief and betrayal. I quickly shake my head, trying to explain myself.

"No, I didn't go through them. I was reaching for my wallet and noticed the open mail and I knocked the mouse, which turned on the screen. But with everything that has happened, the failed deal, and the issues with the scones, I let my fear get the best of me."

Her expression softens slightly, but there is still a hint of anger in her eyes. "For the last time, Connor Abernathy. I did not curse your scones or give you a love potion. I'm sorry that your deal didn't work out, but it had nothing to do with me." Her voice is firm, and her cheeks flush with frustration.

Connor.

"I didn't—" I try to interject, but she cuts me off, her voice filled with exasperation.

"You didn't? You didn't storm into my job demanding I

remove the curse I supposedly placed on you? You didn't keep coming to find me even after I explained the truth?" I feel a pang of guilt and frustration as I realize the extent of my actions.

Realizing my mistake, I curse under my breath, my hands involuntarily clenching at my sides. "I was wrong," I admit, my voice filled with regret. "I shouldn't have resorted to magic in the first place. I let my fears and insecurities get the best of me."

Her anger seems to dissipate, replaced by a cold and hardened expression. Her shoulders slump, and she speaks with a hint of resignation. "Just go back to your business and your life," she says, her voice laced with sadness. I watch helplessly as she turns away, her disappointment palpable.

"Netti, I don't want to go back to that life, alone. As soon as I left you, I felt deep down that I was being an ass and should go back." I run a hand frustrated through my hair.

"Then why didn't you?" Her voice cracks, tears rimming her green eyes.

"I couldn't." I rub my chest where a deep ache resonates. "I was on the phone with Carter, about to turn around, when the car broke down. Since the day I met you, anytime I've left your side, bad things happen."

"So, you're implying I've put a hex on you—that you'll suffer if you try to leave me?" She lets out a short, choked laugh, a sound more like a hiccup than genuine amusement as she shakes her head in disbelief. "You're ridiculous."

"No, I don't think you put a hex on me. I don't know what is going on, but I do know one thing for certain. If you'll have me, I want you in my life." I grab her face between my hands, pressing our foreheads together and inhaling her sweet vanilla chai scent. "I want to see where this goes—where we go."

She's silent, her shoulders rising and falling with each breath until she opens her eyes and looks at me.

"You can be such a grumpy ass sometimes," she says, her voice barely a whisper.

"I know." I go to drop my hands, but she wraps her hands around my wrists, stilling me. She breaks my gaze to glance at the sky. I follow her gaze, seeing the full moon in the bright afternoon sun.

"And bossy," she adds, returning to meet my gaze.

"I know." I hang my head.

"But... I do want to try this thing between us out." The corners of her lips curl up into a small smile.

"You do?" My heart leaps in my chest, and if I had been in my wolven form, my tail would have been wagging like a pup.

"Yes, Connor. But with a couple of requirements. We're going to be a team. No more jumping to conclusions."

Kiss her and grovel, you dick.

"Deal." I lean in, my breath catching in my throat, and capture her lips in a kiss that is both demanding and tender.

She pulls back, her lips swollen and cheeks flushed. The urge to scoop her up and carry her somewhere where we can be alone is overwhelming, but I fight it, knowing it's not the most civilized approach.

"What about your company and the deal with Summit?" she asks breathlessly.

"Forget the deal with Summit. I've been working my entire life, always searching for something. I put that energy into growing Abernathy Inc. and helping the pack from afar."

A gruff, masculine voice pierces through my thoughts, snapping me back to reality as I remember my brother and Netti's best friend standing there, watching and waiting.

Jealousy flares, hot and sharp, and I spin to face him, my body instinctively positioning itself between Carter and Netti.

"Unless you want to take me up on my proposal." He pushes off the car, heading toward us as he rolls up his shirt sleeves. "Or we could let fate decide what should have happened decades ago."

"Leave Netti out of this." I hold my stance.

"Why? Jealous, Connor? Afraid if she spends too much time with the pack, she will find a mate before you claim her?"

His body morphs, teeth sharpening and claws extending from his hands. It's all the warning I get before he transforms into a giant dark brown wolf and lunges for us. Red hot fury momentarily blinds me, and my body morphs on its own accord, meeting Carter mid-air and tackling him to the ground. I twist as his jaw snaps at my neck, narrowly missing. We back up, teeth bared and growling as we circle each other.

We are nearly identical in our wolf forms, except he is leaner than I last recall. My eyes scan his body when I notice a slight limp in his left paw, and I seize the opportunity. I pounce, knocking him to the ground and forcing the left forepaw to buckle beneath him. Growling, I snap at his neck, my sharp teeth barely biting into his flesh and fur.

Suddenly, I am filled with a rush of power that leaves me feeling dizzy. I stumble back, fur turning into flesh, and I fall to my knees. Carter's body morphs back into his human form, and he lays on the ground naked, laughing. He lifts a hand to his neck and stares at the small smear of blood on his palm.

As I catch my breath, the realization of what transpired settles in. Carter, my once-trusted friend and brother, attacked me and my mate. But why? What was going on?

I quickly gather my wits and stand, keeping a cautious distance from him. The air is heavy with tension, and the silence is broken only by our heavy breaths as we stare at each other.

I can't help but feel a pang of guilt as I look at the blood on his hand. It's my blood, drawn by my teeth. The taste of victory is bittersweet, knowing I have wounded someone I once cared deeply for.

"Why did you do that?"

"I knew you had it in you, Alpha," Carter says as he stands, pulls on his pants, and offers me a hand.

Alpha.

The rush of power I am feeling suddenly makes sense. By beating him in outright combat over pack and mate, his wolf had bowed in submission, and the Alpha magic transferred to me.

"You tricked me," I say, stunned and looking at his offered hand.

"No, you bested me. Now, you have the pack and the girl," Carter says as he helps me to my feet and inclines his head respectfully.

"What is going on here?" Netti steps to my side, my clothes bundled up in her arms. Rose stands smugly beside her, staring at my brother.

"What did he mean by claim me?"

Her green eyes turned to meet mine, and I feel the insistent pull to protect her, claim her.

"He—"

"Connor is your mate. Your life partner. When a shifter finds their mate and accepts the bond, they give them a mating mark so any shifters you come across know that you're taken."

"That sounds painful." Netti touches her neck.

"It's more of a magical mark, not a physical one. Although traditionally, it was both. Most packs no longer uphold the physical marring of flesh." Carter shrugs, and Netti wraps her arms around her middle. "It explains his obsessive attraction to you when you first met that he blankly ignored and blamed on your scones instead." Carter points between the two of us. "I could smell him on you the moment I met you, and I knew by the way your scents had entwined that he had unintentionally marked you as his, but I saw no mating mark."

"That's because I don't want Netti to be forced into a relationship determined by fate," I say, my voice tight with anger as I yank my shirt over my head and shove it into my pants.

"It's because you were in denial that she is your mate," Carter retorts. His words feel like a punch in my gut.

If you would have just listened to me...

"What I want to know is how both of you managed to change forms without ripping a single piece of fabric," Rose says, her touch lingering on the crisp cotton of Carter's shirt. The warmth of her touch seems to radiate through him, and I watch as he nearly melts under her touch, his whole body relaxing.

"Magic. Especially as children learning to control the shift, if our clothes weren't enchanted, we'd have nothing left to wear," I explain.

"What do you mean Connor now has the pack? Aren't you the pack leader?" Netti's brows furrow together and she nibbles on her bottom lip. "What does that mean about your offer?"

"The clan still needs a healer," Carter says as he shrugs.

"I cannot be the Alpha. That is—" My phone vibrates in Netti's hands where she still holds my belt and wallet, cutting off my words.

"I'm sorry I didn't want them trampled." She shoves my things toward me.

"It's not important," I mutter, reaching for the phone, but my hand stops as I glance at the caller ID.

Summit Contracting Group.

"Answer it," Netti gently encourages.

"Connor? This is Rogers. I've stumbled upon some intriguing news, and I'm eager to share it with you while we discuss your proposal in more detail."

CHAPTER 15
CONNOR

"How did your meeting go?" Netti asks from across the table at EnchanTea.

"I haven't seen your beautiful face in nearly three weeks and the first thing you want to talk about is how my work is doing?" I raise an eyebrow as my thumb rubs lazy circles on the back of her hand.

"Well, I did offer you to meet me at my place," she says with a wry grin. "But need I remind you that it was you who wanted to meet up for breakfast and coffee first?"

I wanted to go with option A at her condo, if you need my opinion.

I clear my throat, ignoring my wolf and the thoughts of Netti spread out before me on this table that he sends.

"That's because I'm trying to show restraint and get to know you. Trust me, having you alone and all to myself is on my agenda for this week." I flip over her hand and kiss the tender skin of her wrist. She lets out a quiet moan, her cheeks flushing red.

"Connor," she says, her eyes glassy with need. "You don't think talking for hours on end every night counts as getting to know each other?"

"Oh, my sweet little mate." I encompass her hand within mine, giving it a squeeze. "I plan on spending the rest of our lives getting to know every inch of you."

"And how long is that?" She raises an eyebrow. "How old are you, exactly Connor Abernathy? Thirty-seven, Thirty-eight?"

"Fifty-six to be exact. Young by wolf shifter standards. We age about half the time that most humans do." I turn and accept the two drinks from the barista and hand Netti her steaming chai tea latte mug.

She blows the steam off the top of her cup, peering at me soberly with a frown. "So I'll grow old and die while you go on to live another half century on me?"

"Oh no, my beautiful nettle." I lean forward and run my thumb across her bottom lip. As my mate, our lifelines are irrevocably tied together and you'll age slower with me."

"What about children?"

I cough, nearly gagging on my black coffee. "Children?"

"Yes, children. Or do you not want children?" She casts her eyes down at the table, nibbling her bottom lip.

"Netti, I want to experience everything with you. If the goddess blesses us with children then I will be overjoyed to add pups to the pack."

Her eyes widen and she sets her mug on the table.

"Did I say something wrong?" My brows furrow together. "If you don't want children, I'm sure Carter will sire plenty of pups–"

"It's not that," she says in a rush. "I want children... in the future. It's just–" She runs a finger along the edge of her mug before meeting my gaze. "Will they be... puppies?"

I toss my head back in laughter before smiling at her. "No, not as infants. They're born just like human babies, although twins are fairly common. They don't manifest their shifter ability until closer to toddlers. I also don't know a lot about halflings. When I was a pup, shifters mostly mated with other shifters. I'm sure any children you bear will be as beautiful as you."

"I think I'd like that. To one day have a family in the future. However, I've got too much on the plate to think about that. Wrapping my mind around being mated–"

"I know. It's a lot to take on."

"Did you know I knew?" She sips at her latte before continuing. "Well, not 100% but I suspected. After our first encounter, I ran into one of my neighbors on the way to work and she had a vision that I had met my mate, which at the time I thought was silly. I knew about soul mates, but I thought only shifters and certain species bonded, not humans and witches. The more you kept coming back and accusing me of messing up the scones–I was torn between wondering if my magic was on the fritz or if she was right."

"Why didn't you say something?"

"Would you have believed me? You thought I'd cursed you to be obsessed with me and lose on your deal. How crazy would it be to hear 'hey by the way, some old witch told me *Catch your mate before the next full moon, or else your life will take a turn down a dangerous path.*"

"You're right. At the time–well, hindsight is 20:20 and I'm never letting you out of my sight again." I finish the rest of my coffee and stand, offering her my hand. "Walk with me? I've got to meet Summit in a couple of hours, but then you've got me all to yourself for the rest of the weekend and I've rented a suite in a bed and breakfast down the street."

"You never answered my question," she says as she finishes her cup and takes my hand.

"Which one?" I ask, pulling her into my arms and pressing a kiss against her lips.

She pulls away breathlessly before waving goodbye to the barista. We head outside into the chilly fall air.

"How did your meeting go? I'm presuming well if he's invited you back." Her fingers intertwine with mine and I feel happiness and love pulsing through the ever stronger golden ribbon tying us together.

"We're still in the early stages of discussion, but it's looking good. That's why I have to go back today." We turn the corner into a clean alley and I pull her to me, threading my free hand through the hair on the back of her head and pinning her against the brick wall. I kiss her until we both pull away, panting with lips swollen.

"You keep kissing me like that and you'll miss your meeting," she says breathlessly as she licks her lips.

"I can't help it that you look so delicious," I growl, my hand moving down her neck and chest to cup her breast as I push my hips against her, my arousal pressing tightly against my dress slacks. "If you keep teasing me, I'll take you right here where everyone can see."

"Connor," she gasps, head falling against the brick as my hand travels further down, pulling her hips against me.

"Just a taste of what you're in for tonight, my little nettle," I growl against the shell of her ear before nipping playfully at her neck. "Just a taste of what you're in for, for our entire life. My mate."

CHAPTER 16

NETTI

"Gods, you are beautiful," Connors whispers seductively against the shell of my ear, sending shivers down my spine. His hands slide around my waist, their warmth seeping through the fabric of my dress and igniting a tingling sensation on my skin as he guides me forward. My heart races with anticipation. "I could spend every day looking at you."

"Then explain why you've been gone for three weeks." I pout even though we've spent every night talking and my body needed the recovery from the last time he was here.

"The same reason you've been busy. I've got work and you've got a degree to finish." His hands gently squeeze mine and he pulls me forward.

"Can I see yet?" My stomach tightens in nervous knots, my vision blocked by the silk handkerchief tied securely around my eyes.

"Patience, little nettle," he murmurs, his lips grazing the sensitive skin on my neck, causing me to gasp in delight. I hear a metallic click, followed by the heavy door opening, and then Connor firmly grasps my hand, his other hand possessively wrapped around my waist, leading me into the room.

As we enter, the enticing aroma of freshly baked goods and the rich scent of freshly brewed coffee fills the air, instantly capturing my senses. Inhaling deeply, I savor the familiar and comforting fragrance. "Stay here," Connor instructs, gently guiding me to sit on a plush chair. I strain my ears, focusing on his steps as he moves around the room.

"Can I have a hint?" I tilt my head to the side, trying to gather any familiar sounds, but apart from the delightful scent of baked goods, my surroundings remain a mystery.

"Open your mouth," Connor demands, his voice commanding yet laced with excitement. A tremor of anticipation runs through me, heightening my senses.

"Excuse me?" I reply, feeling a surge of arousal at his authoritative tone.

"Be a good girl and open your mouth," he repeats, his warm breath brushing against my cheek like a gentle caress. Heat surges between my thighs, spreading throughout my body, as I obediently part my lips, waiting for what awaits me. A cold, smooth object brushes against my lips, and instinctively, I dip out my tongue. The sweet taste of chocolate melts at the touch, and I eagerly bite down, savoring the sweetness and the tang of strawberries that explode in my mouth. The juice drips onto the top of my breasts, a tantalizing sensation against my heated skin.

"Fuck," Connor growls, his voice filled with desire. The scruff of his beard grazes against my skin as he dips his head down to lick the strawberry juice. "No one should look that fucking sexy eating a chocolate-covered strawberry."

A breathless reply escapes my lips as I try to touch him, but he firmly grasps my wrists and guides them back to the armrests.

"Not yet," he murmurs. His hands glide up my arms, across my shoulders, and deftly unzip the back of my dress. With a skillful touch, he rolls the fabric down to my waist, revealing my bare breasts. The cool air of the room causes my nipples to pebble, and my head falls back in pleasure as Connor takes one breast into his mouth, his other hand firmly gripping the flesh, kneading and pinching the sensitive nipple.

"Connor," I beg, squeezing my thighs together in an attempt to assuage the growing ache at my center.

He pulls away, leaving me longing for his touch. I whine softly, feeling the sudden absence. But then he slowly kneels between my legs, the cool air brushing against my exposed skin. He removes my boots, his hands gliding up the back of my calves. The sensation sends shivers up my spine.

His fingers continue their deliberate path, trailing higher along my bare thighs. I can feel the pressure as he pushes my skirt, exposing more of my skin. The scent of his cologne mingles with the faint aroma of the chocolate strawberries. My anticipation builds as I feel him squeeze my thighs, holding them open.

He dips his head, his warm breath caressing my most intimate area. The delicate lace tickles against my sensitive skin, adding a teasing sensation.

"This is all I've been able to think about all day," he growls in a husky voice, making my heart race. In one swift motion, he grabs the waistband of my panties and rips them off.

Without hesitation, his mouth is on me. He feasts with a hunger and urgency that ignites a fire within me. I can't help but cry out, my hands instinctively flying to his head and tangling in his short, dark hair as his fingers dig into my thighs, causing a mix of pleasure and pain.

"Connor," I gasp, my voice filled with feral desire. The chair beneath me becomes a battleground of sensations as I writhe and squirm with each lick, suck, and growl that escapes from him.

A surge of heat courses through my veins, making me feel like I'm about to burst from my skin. The pleasure becomes almost unbearable, and I rock against his mouth, desperately seeking more. My need for him intensifies with every second; my body and mind are consumed by a primal hunger. I rock against his mouth, pulling him closer, desperate for more of this feeling he was building inside me. More of him.

"That's it, my nettle. Take your pleasure from me. Come for me." His voice is a low, throaty growl.

He releases my hips, reaching one hand up my chest to play with my nipple as he continues to stroke my center with his tongue and circle my clit with his thumb.

The sensations are nearly too much to bear. I might die right here.

"I want you to look at me when you find your release." His voice vibrates against my core, and I squeeze my legs around his head. He releases my nipple and pulls the silk down over my face, stroking my bottom lip with his thumb. "You. Are. Mine."

He picks up his tempo, then slides his finger inside me. My release crashes through me, my core clenching around his finger as waves of pleasure consume me. I cry out and arch in the chair against his mouth as my head rolls back.

A low growl resonates in his chest, and his grip tightens around my hips. He kisses me once more between my legs before standing, placing his hands on either armrest, caging me within them.

"You don't have to choose me now. We have time. But I want you to be mine. I want to prove myself worthy of you."

He stands and scoops me up in his arms. My eyes drink in the stunning sight before me. The room is adorned with flickering candlelight from dozens of candles, casting a warm and romantic glow. Vibrant colors of red and gold dance across the walls, creating an atmosphere of opulence. Delicate flower arrangements grace every surface, adding a touch of elegance to the house.

"Connor, this is beautiful. What is this place?" I turn to face him in his arms. We hadn't traveled long enough to be out of town, but this didn't look like a hotel or a bed and breakfast.

"Summit wants me to stay in town for a few weeks or longer while we settle some plans. I figured renting a place would let me attend those meetings and be close to you." He grins and presses a quick kiss to my lips. "I thought it would give you some space to still be yourself, but we could slowly learn each other. You're welcome to come and go as you please. Stay here full-time if you like. There are plenty of rooms."

"But what about your business?" I nibble at my bottom lip and wrap my arms around his neck.

"They'll survive without me for a few weeks. It's about time they operate without me there every hour of every day. Plus, I'll need to move to the pack now and see what my brother has been up to." He carries me through a door into a large room with floor-to-ceiling windows and a large claw tub sitting before them.

I peer out the window at the lake and treeline spotted a few houses a few hundred yards away.

My body stiffens as I remember I don't have a scrap of clothing on me, but Connor nuzzles against the side of my head and whispers. "It's coated so no one can see in, only out."

"Connor, this is... beautiful." He sets me on my feet, and I run my fingers over the edge of the tub. He turns on the faucets, steam billowing in the air.

"You deserve it and so much more." He pours oil from a glass bottle into the tub, filling the room with the sweet smell of vanilla and bergamot. He takes my hand and leads me into the water, the heat of the water rushing over my skin until I'm submerged up to my shoulders. "I know you have final exams tomorrow, and I wanted to make sure you didn't spend the weekend stressing over them."

"I wouldn't have—" He lifts a brow, and I shut my mouth. We'd only known each other for a couple of weeks, and already he knew me and my habits.

"Plus, I wanted to talk to you about your winter break. Carter has asked us to join him for the festivities, but I know your parents aren't too far away..." He trails off, warm hands coated in oil running along my shoulders and neck. He works his way through the knots in my back, kneading deep, slow circles that send shivers down my spine. I lean into his touch, letting out a low groan of pleasure.

"I'm off from the university but still have to work at the bakery." I lean my head back and peek open an eye at him. He leans forward and kisses my brow.

"It's already taken care of. The shop owner said you had more PTO than you knew what to do with, and they've already hired extra holiday help that will more than cover your shifts."

"But what about—"

Connor nuzzles the side of my head before kissing my cheek. "We both work too hard and deserve the break. Plus, you need the mental rest before you start your last semester."

"If we are both working too hard, how come I'm the only one in this giant tub that can fit at least four people?" I roll over, winking and flicking water in his direction. He flinches and ducks. "Or are wolves afraid of water?"

"Oh, you little vixen." My eyes skim the firm muscles that bulge and flex as Connor strips off his clothes. He settles into the tub, the water splashing over the sides as his body presses against mine, the warmth of his skin a welcome embrace. "Wolves love water."

"Is that so?" I lift my hands from the water and run them down his chest. He closes his eyes, a deep rumble in his chest.

"Yes, but I like looking at you in the water better," Connor whispers seductively in my ear. As his hand slips between my thighs, a shiver runs down my spine, anticipation building within me. His touch is electric, his thumb caressing my clit in slow, tantalizing circles.

I can't help but gasp, my body arching toward him, craving more of his intoxicating touch. With a skillful movement, he slips a finger inside me, and the sensation sends waves of pleasure coursing through my body. My fingers instinctively dig into his shoulders, my breaths coming in shallow gasps as he adds another digit, stretching me open.

"Connor," I moan, unable to control the desire in my voice. I pull his face down to mine. Our lips meet in a hungry and possessive kiss, our tongues intertwining in a passionate dance. At that moment, I realize his expertise and mastery extend beyond his touch between my legs—his kisses are equally as intense and mind-blowing.

"Come for me, Netti." He increases his tempo, and I arch, lost to the sensations building inside me. He kisses down the side of my face, his teeth grazing the delicate skin of my neck. My heart pounds in my chest, my breathing ragged. I cry out as waves of pleasure course through me. "Good girl." He nips at my neck before flipping both of us around so that he's lounging in the water and I'm straddled on top of him, my breasts barely above the water.

"What—" I brace my hands on either side of him. He stares at me hungrily, his wolf shimmering in the depths of his eyes.

"Ride me," he commands, his fingers gripping my hips and

lifting me. His length is hard and thick, probing at my entrance. He leans forward, catching a nipple in his mouth as he pushes me down. He groans against my breast, his tongue flicking my nipple as he fills me. My head falls back, hands clenching the side of the tub as my body adjusts to him.

"Oh, Connor." I move my hips, slowly at first before picking up the tempo. My breathing becomes steadier, faster as we move in perfect unison. His hands squeeze my hips, and with a deep thrust, he pushes fully inside me. I cry out.

His hands gently trace the outline of my bun, then, with a light pull, send my hair cascading into the water. He claims my mouth with his as he rolls his hips again. I reach out and hook my fingers around his neck, pulling him closer and allowing myself to be completely vulnerable in his embrace.

"I've wanted this for so long. I've wanted you like this for so long." He growls into my ear. He dips his mouth to my throat, where he kisses, sucks, and nibbles.

I grab his face. His jawline is tight, and again, I see the glimmer of his wolf barely restrained in his eyes.

"Take what you want from me. I want to give it to you," I whisper.

"Netti—" His voice is strained as he pauses his movements, holding me tightly as though any moment I'm going to float again. "I want to give you time. You don't know what you're—"

"I am not afraid. This is my choice. This is what I want." I grind my hips against his before tilting my head to the side in submission. I've been thinking about it and made my choice days ago.

He growls and plunges into me hard. His teeth sink into the side of my neck, and I feel the sharp pain shoot through me. The bite explodes with a burst of magic, making me tense and cry out in surprise. Around us, bottles of shampoo, oils, a bar of soap and a stack of towels levitate in the air.

"Fuck. Sorry." He pulls back, but I shake my head and meet his gaze.

"Take it, take me," I nearly growl. I'd never had an outburst of magic like that, but I'd deal with that later. I tilt my hips to take him deeper, desperate for more of him. I slide my hands down his back, urging him further inside.

"Who's the bossy one now?" A chuckle escapes his lips as he lifts me from the water, the scent of the oils clinging to me. He carries me to the other room and lays me down on a king-size four-poster bed, the grey silk sheets feeling luxurious against my skin.

"I know what I want," I say, the corners of my lips curling up into a small smile.

"Good, because I'll never be done with you." With a powerful thrust, he enters me again, the sensation hitting me hard and deep. I instinctively wrap my legs around his back, drawing him closer. The change in pressure and friction provokes delicious tension within me.

"Look at me, Netti," Connor murmurs.

I bring my eyes back to his. He plunges into me and it pushes me over the edge. Release surges through me, and I cry out, arching up against him as I come completely undone. His movements become feverish and frenzied as he picks up pace. Then he groans, and I feel him spasm inside me as he spills deep in me.

"Fuck, Netti." He says as he collapses beside me and pulls me into his arms. He leans down, his lips brushing gently against my forehead before pulling a thick, soft blanket over us.

"You're mine."

EPILOGUE
The Chrismas Kiss

"The maroon house on the left." I point down the street toward the charming Cape Cod-style house with smoke curling from the chimney. The roofline is outlined with twinkling Christmas lights, and the two tall pines in front of the house are wrapped in strings of lights like shimmering emerald giants.

Connor pulls his sleep navy blue electric car up to the front of the house and puts it in park. He pushes up the sleeves on his sweater with "Happy Howlidays" and a wolf howling at a moon on the front before straightening them again.

"Don't worry, Mom and Dad are going to love you." I lay a hand on his forearm and lean over before kissing his cheek. "If you can lead a whole pack of wolves, you can handle one Christmas dinner with a handful of witches."

"Is that so?" He raises an eyebrow before pulling me close and pressing a kiss to my lips that leaves me breathless.

"It's not like you're going to huff and puff and blow their

house down to eat them." I snort and slap him playfully across the chest.

"No," he says with a smirk, his eyes flickering with desire. "But there are definitely other things to eat I have in mind." As he slides his hand under the hem of my sweater, a rush of warmth floods through me.

"Connor," I gasp, writhing in my seat. I cast a glance through the windows to the front of the house. "Someone could see."

"I know, I know." He chuckles and presses a quick kiss to my lips. He gets out of the car and comes around to the passenger side, letting me out and offering me a hand.

"Netti!" Mom's voice calls, and I turn to wave at her standing in the front door, apron around her waist. Her silvery brown hair is pulled into a neat bun atop her head. Connor grabs our bags from the trunk, hands me the box of baked goods, and follows me up the drive with one hand on the small of my back.

"Hi, Mom," I greet her as she approaches.

She pulls me into a warm hug, and I inhale her familiar butterscotch scent, instantly feeling at home. "Oh, I've missed you, honey," she says, holding me at arm's length and examining me closely. "You've changed so much."

"I don't think a couple of years at school has changed me that much, Mom," I reply with a chuckle. She steps back and turns her attention to Connor, giving him a thorough appraisal. "This young man must be your Connor," she remarks, a hint of playfulness in her tone.

"Yes, ma'am," Connor responds, flashing her a charming smile and extending his hand. "It's a pleasure to meet you, Mrs. Ellsworth."

"Oh, nonsense," Mom dismisses, pulling him into a warm embrace. I give Connor a thumbs up, barely hiding my amusement as she turns and leads him into the house. "Now you call me Mom. The two of you look nearly starved. Your brothers and father are out back smoking a ham, but why don't you two come into the kitchen and get a cup of warm cider and some snacks?" she suggests warmly.

Honey flaps his wings on top of my head, and Mom gives his head a little pet. "It's good to see you too, Honey. You don't think your grandmama would have forgotten about you. I made a special treat just for you," she croons.

With a grateful nod, we follow Mom into the welcoming aroma of home-cooked food. Connor gives my hand a reassuring squeeze.

"You can put your bags here. I'll have one of the boys take them to your room." Mom gestures to a bench by the door. "Or did you want separate?"

"One room is fine," I reply in a rush, my cheeks heating.

"I figured as much. I might be old, but your dad and I were young and in love once. Well, we're still in love, just not as young as we once were." We reach the kitchen, and Mom busies herself making drinks.

"Is there anything I can help with?" I set the box of baked goods on the table with the other appetizers. In the corner is the Christmas tree decorated with hundreds of sparkling lights and tinsel. Christmas music plays from a smaller speaker in the kitchen, and the entire house smells like cinnamon and nutmeg.

"Yeah, you can explain why you've let a dog in the house," Harrison says as he hobbles over, one foot in a boot. He slings an arm around me and punches me playfully in my shoulder. "Run away from us to go to some fancy schmancy school and come home with a new pet."

"Harrison!" I slip from his grasp and pinch his arm. "Don't be rude."

He waves me away in mock hurt. Ethan and Matthew come through the back door next, followed by Dad. The two of them drop right into grilling Connor about his job, his hobbies, and his intentions. I break free from Harrison and slip my arm through Connor's.

"Connor, this is Ethan, Matthew, and Harrison, my brothers." I glance around the room before looking pointedly at Harrison. "Is Poppy Marie joining us for dinner?"

He drops my gaze, turning ten shades of red as he toes the carpet.

"Are you boys trampling in mud from outside on my newly mopped floor?" Mom chides as she walks over, carrying two steaming mugs of spiked spiced cider. She hands them to Connor and me. I take a sip, relishing in the sweet taste.

"Mom, did you hear Netti's new boyfriend's pack is only a short drive south of us?" Ethan says, distracting her as he leads her back into the kitchen.

"Is that so, Netti? What does that mean for graduation and your career?" She glances between the two of us.

"Well, our pack healer is looking to bring on nurses to train as the pack is growing, and we are starting to expand beyond shifters to humans, fae, and other creatures." He caresses the back of my hand with his thumb. "Until then, I've purchased a rental house in Rusthollow while I finish a business contract and Netti finishes her courses."

"Is this what you want, Netti?" Mom looks at me, worry and concern in her eyes.

"Netti only ever does what she wants," Matthew and Ethan chime in, pulling up to stand on either side of Connor, eyeing him speculatively.

Dad wraps his arms around Mom and kisses her on the forehead.

"The ham should be done in about an hour." He turns to face us and offers out his hand.

"It's a pleasure to meet you, Mr. Abernathy," Dad says, shaking his proffered hand.

"Please, it's Connor."

"Harrison, could you get the spare chairs from the attic?" Mom asks as she chops up vegetables and adds them to a tray.

"We can get them," I chime in, dragging Connor to the stairs. "Harrison should probably put his foot up, and we need to put our bags in our room.

Connor hefts our bags, the weight of them settling on his shoulders, and we climb the stairs.

"This is where we will stay—" I turn around, and Connor, with a look of pure adoration, cups my face in his hands and kisses me deeply.

"You're so beautiful." There is a playful glint in his eyes. He kisses the tip of my nose, then my mouth. He looks down at me with a slow, loving smile.

I can't help the grin from spreading across my face, a feeling of elation bubbling inside me.

"Netti Ellsworth." Connor falls to his knees and pulls a box from his back pocket, opening it to reveal a small rose gold ring with a singular diamond shining in the middle. "You've taken me as your mate, but will you be my wife?"

"Connor." I gasp before falling into his embrace and wrapping my arms around his neck. "Yes. Yes, a hundred times, yes."

"Good, now let me show you how much you mean to me." He pushes the door closed with the tip of his foot and lowers me to the ground before covering my body with his. His pants are stretched taut by his obvious arousal, making it impossible to ignore.

"Connor! My parents and brothers are downstairs," I hiss

as his hand slips up my skirt and teases me through my lace underwear, sliding them down my thighs.

"Then we will just have to be quick, and you'll have to be quiet." He strokes me, and I moan, pressing my head back against the floor. His body is warm above me, and his fingers stroke a fire deep in my center.

"So wet, so ready for me," Connor growls as he nips my ear with his teeth, sending a surge of pleasure running through me.

"Then what's taking so long?" My hips lift, seeking more friction. With one swift moment, he frees his erection, rolls on a condom, and lines himself up to my entrance.

"Oh," I gasp as he pushes himself deep, the sensation over-whelming all other thoughts. His eyes flash golden as he runs slow, excruciating circles with his thumb. Pleasure hums through me as he thrusts faster and harder. He catches my mouth in a hungry kiss as I cry out as unending pleasure floods me in waves. His hand tangles in my hair, pulling tight as he thrusts one last time, his erection pulsing deep inside.

"Merry Christmas, darling," he whispers as he presses a kiss to my temple.